One for S
Two for

C000148725

Dorothy M Mitchell

chipmunkapublishing
the mental health publisher

Dorothy M Mitchell

Published by
Chipmunkapublishing
PO Box 6872
Brentwood
Essex CM13 1ZT
United Kingdom

http://www.chipmunkapublishing.com

Chipmunkapublishing gratefully acknowledge the support of Arts Council England.

One for Sorrow Two for Joy

Hello Folks

I was born in a small village just before the start of World War 2. I have vivid memories as I grew up, of being in the air raid shelter as enemy bombers filled the sky, the droning noise as the flew above our house was pretty scary, I can't say at the age of six, I really understood the situation, but sensed that things were pretty awful. I remember my mum, swapping clothing coupons for food ones, this was a regular occurrence at that time, one of my most vivid memories, was the fact, that you couldn't get sweets or chocolate in our sweet shop on the corner of our street, the jars were empty.

We moved to Evesham in 1953. My dad, had got the job of steward to the Working Men's Club. It took a bit of adjustment. I missed my village in Yorkshire, but As mum said; it was dad's work, and that was that.

I met my first husband at the age of seventeen. I married at eighteen, we were together for thirty six years, I have two wonderful sons and seven grandchildren. When I was thirty six I was diagnosed with MULTIPLE Sclerosis. The first two years were a nightmare of attacks to different parts of my body and a degree of mental trauma, .attacks happen still, the trigeminal verve in my jaw being the favourite target

My husband died at the age of fifty eight and I was devastated, my boys were very good, but they both have families of their own, about a year after his death, I met an acquaintance who asked my if I would like to go to her church the following Sunday, my thought at that time, was 'why not' I can't feel any worse than I do right now. So off I went. That was the start of my new life, The Pastor of the church spoke to me, the people were nice, I cried out my pain.

There was a man in church who had lost his wife to illness a year before I was widowed and, all in church were worried about him he appeared to be going down and down. Well to cut a long story short we fell in love and married seventeen years ago. Two years after we wed, poetry started to come into my life, I found making up rhymes easy. This was followed by my writing books for children, over the past few years I have managed to have three novels and various poetry books published. My husband Ken, my Son's Andrew and David, my Grandson Ben have guided me through thus far my thanks also go to THE INSPIRA GROUP and DARIN JEWELL, M D. My dream is to carry on writing, I am not able to do a great deal now, but my writing takes me to out of the mundane, and into flights of fancy.

Please enjoy my novel

DOROTHY M MITCHELL

CHAPTER 1

MAGPIES ROOST AND ROSES

Ruth Jennings was awakened by the sound of the blacksmith's hammer as it made contact with the anvil. Each blow ringing like a bell. She gave a contented sigh, jumped out of bed, and walked over to the bedroom window, there he was, Bill Jobson, doing what he always did. Six days a week would find Bill either shoeing one of Jim Flint's horses, or mending a wrought iron gate or two. Perhaps, on a Sunday afternoon, he could be found in his smithy drinking from his cider mug, liked his cider did old Bill. Mind you, he reckoned that St. Peters Church was a must on a Sunday morning, his loud baritone voice shaking the rafters of the old church.
"Does me good to talk to him upstairs, puts me right for the week ahead." Jim tells anyone who cares to listen. Ruth had listened and smiled, she liked Bill Jobson.
The man had doffed his cap to her more than once, she wasn't interested, he was a nice enough man, but the thought of him touching her made the girl shudder.

Ruth watched as the blacksmith lifted the cartwheel he'd just been working on, the girl thought his arms resembled tree trunks and his hands, well, they reminded her of the meat pasties her Granny made. Would she miss this place when she and Reuben wed and moved into Magpies Roost? The answer was yes, but as her new home when she married Reuben Ford, was situated the other side of the Bill Jobson Smithy, then she supposed it wouldn't be so bad. She would still hear the magpie's wheezing, chittering squawk early on a summers morning as they also, were awakened by the blacksmiths hammering.

The village of Applebee was in the East Riding of Yorkshire, about one and a half miles from Hull. A pretty hamlet with a scattering of dwellings, two churches, one school, three sprawling farms, and a doctor by the name of Samuel De Witt. Ruth liked him, he had been kind to her mum during the illness, accepting in kind, a few eggs or an apple pie in exchange for treatment administered.

Fortunately, Kate Jennings, Ruth's mother, seemed quite fit again and busy preparing for the big day; she was looking forward to the May wedding,
Ruth, however, was a little concerned about her mum, she never said much, but the girl knew about the pain her mother tried to cover up. Her heart wasn't as strong as she made out, Ruth had watched as Kate struggled to breathe on many occasions.

"A nice time to get wed Lass." She'd said to Ruth, "Eighteen's a bit young, but Reuben Ford is a good Lad, and you won't be far away."

Ruth was fond of her Mam, and she would miss living in this cottage, but she comforted herself with the thought that her new home was only be two doors away, she could pop in every day and make sure her Mam and Dad were alright.

May 1903 arrived. Ruth awoke to a bright morning, she stretched, and yawned, and as she lay looking up at the ceiling, a shadow came across her face. She was happy, of course she was, in a few hours she would be Mrs Ruth Ford, but this little cottage had been her home since she was baby.

Ruth hadn't been the only child to Kate and Eli Jennings, there had been another girl but Ruby had died of consumption at the age of three. This had almost broken her parents, Ruth could only vaguely remember the tragedy, her being about five at the time, but she remembered the wooden box, and the crying.

"Come on Ruth, time to get up love." Her mother called up the stairs. Ruth pushed the rough blankets back, and almost reluctantly left the comfy flock mattress, she was happy however that the feather pillows her mother had made for her, would be going with her to Magpie's Roost, her new home.

Ruth poured a jug of water into the wash bowl removed her night-shirt, and began to wash, being careful not to wet the strips of rag that her mother had laboriously tied into her thick dark hair. Ruth didn't care for this much, feeling the bits of cloth tended to pinch her neck, but she had to admit, that the ringlets were rather fetching, especially when tied up with pink ribbon.

"Breakfast's on the table Lass, Martha laid you a nice brown egg this morning, special." Her dad was sitting at the old, well-scrubbed table. Ruth walked in to the kitchen. She went over to her father and planted a kiss on his cheek.

Eli gave his daughter that lovely toothless smile, he gazed appraisingly at her, and thought how much like her mam she had become, same dark hair, slim figure and the dark blue eyes that set off her elfish face. Not so elfish now in her mother's case, but then, Kate was older and the suffering was still evident in her careworn features.

Ruth sat down and looked at the brown egg, she couldn't eat it. "Sorry Mam, I can't, my tummy is too churned up." She said. Kate sighed, "You can't get married on an empty stomach love, now come on; try a bit of bread and butter." Her Dad spoke up now with one of his choice comments, "You don't want to be farting in church cos you've got an empty belly my girl, now please do as your Mam says, and have a bite to eat." Ruth chuckled at her Dads comment, took a small portion of bread, nibbled at it and excused herself. How she would miss these moments. This was her wedding day and she would be moving into Magpies Roost later this evening. It would be the first night with her new husband, Reuben Ford.... Ruth felt a shiver run through her body.

Kate looked at her daughter, dressed now in her wedding finery, "You look lovely,
Ruth. The frock is perfect, and I'm glad you chose forget-me-nots and rosebuds to adorn your head-dress, the bouquet goes so well with it."

St. Peters church was looking beautiful, the late spring sunshine flooding through the stained glass windows, bathing the wedding guests in a soft variable light of pale pink, yellow and green. A shaft of pure golden glow seemed to envelope the Bride and Groom in a caress, as they stood in front of Reverend Stanhope who was performing the ceremony. As they took their solemn vows to love and cherish each other for the rest of their lives, little did they know,that married life for them would be fraught with many troubles for some time to come.

The wedding feast had been prepared in Farmer Wickets barn, the farm being Reuben Ford's place of work. He had been employed there since leaving school at the age of   fourteen. The pay wasn't much, but he had been able to supplement it with a part time job at Wheelers Grange.

Kate and friends had worked hard to ensure that everything went with a swing, Grace Wickets had made a beautiful wedding cake, along with an assortment of pies and pastries and sweetmeats. She and Jethro, her husband, had grown fond of the lad, and if the truth was known, Grace Wickets tended to treat Reuben like the son she'd never had. Jethro Wickets had noted this fact, but kept his council anyway. Perhaps the fault was his? They had both wanted children in the early days of their marriage, but despite a normal life, in that way, Grace had never become pregnant.

There was to be a barn dance and a pig roast in the evening, and it went without saying that Eli Jennings along with a few of his cronies got suitably pie eyed, drinking too deeply from the barrel of cider.

About half way through the evening's festivities, Reuben and Ruth slipped away to their new home. They wanted to be together, it had been a long day, and exciting, beautiful, in some ways rather magical, but they needed to be alone. Reuben's need to love his new wife was becoming unbearable; soon Ruth would be his, in the true sense of the word. They had come pretty close to the real thing, on more that one occasion, but because of his deep respect for his girl;, Reuben had been able to hold back, contenting himself with the fact that he hadn't sullied their love outside wedlock.

As for Ruth, well, her being a virgin; was going to the marriage bed with a feeling of trepidation, she had never been with a man and the thought of being touched down there was a bit frightening! She knew how she felt in that private place when Reuben held her tight, his breathing heavy, it was a nice scary feeling, but now they would be sleeping in the same bed, all night...

Magpies Roost was stones throw from Wickets farm. You could say the setting was rather romantic, a tiny stone cottage, situated beside the old Smithy. At this time of year, the roses round the door of Magpies Roost were in bud. They would blossom and form, through to autumn. Ruth would pick the sweet flowers and festoon the cottage with the fragrance. This was to be the pattern, until that fateful autumn day when War, and lives would change forever.

Ruth and Reuben walked along the stony path, the moon was high and full, all was quiet except for the hooting of an owl as it glided over-head having, no doubt, spotted its next meal scurrying in the hay field that was situated to the right of

Magpies Roost. They arrived at the cottage door and stepped inside. Reuben rubbed his hands together, "Come on love, I see the fire your father laid earlier, is still aglow, how about we boil a pan of water on the embers, and have a cup of tea before we go to bed?" Ruth nodded, "A cup of tea would be nice thank you." Why did she feel so shy? She and Reuben had known each other since school days, seeking each other out from all the other children in the village, it was a forgone conclusion that they would marry, everyone expected it and here they were man and wife at last. Reuben put a comforting arm around Ruth, "You alright love?" He asked. Ruth nodded shyly. The newly weds climbed the narrow staircase to the bedroom, and their new lives as man and wife.

They soon got used to living in Magpies Roost. Ruth loved her little cottage, and was happy that she was able to keep an eye on her parent's. It was also a comfort, to still be in earshot of the Blacksmith. Bill Jobson was a good neighbour, if a troubled one and was to prove his worth, further down the line. The man gave no indication that he was jealous of Reuben being the husband of the girl he cared for. But the blacksmith never did marry.

In the summer of 1905, 10th July, to be exact, baby Joe Ford was born, weighing in at eight pound seven ounces. Ruth and Reuben were over the moon, doting on their son with all the love they could give him, but as young Joe grew and developed, it was pretty obvious to anyone who knew him, that his father was young Joe's hero.

During Reuben's spare time away from his job at Wicket's Farm he and the boy were to be found taking care of the precious pigeons. Joe especially enjoyed this job, musing to himself as he stroked them or cleaned their boxes. That if, what his father told him was true, that these birds could in fact find their way home from anywhere, they must be pretty special.

One for Sorrow Two for Joy

Joe enjoyed the stories his father told him about the den in the woods, and he had pestered his Dad to take him to see the now overgrown hideaway for himself. Reuben had been happy to comply with his son's wish to see the construction he had spent many a happy time playing there himself. What Joe found so fascinating about the tale, was the fact that his mam, as a girl, used to play in the den along with his dad and other children, and his Granddad Eli had helped with the building of it.

It had only taken one trip to the den to convince Joe that this was a special place. He found a fascination, with the fact that from the path, nobody would know anything of the special place. Joe remembered feeling awe-struck, the first time he set eyes on the den even under mountains of undergrowth, though the entrance was still accessible.
Bluebell wood was very dense, about ten acres in all, a perfect place to play and discover things.

This story always made Joe feel good inside. His Mam and Dad growing up together, made him feel safe somehow…little did the lad know of the disaster that was to befall him, or that the den would feature so strongly in his life.

Fishing in Spooner's brook, bird nesting, or whittling wood in the back garden of Magpies Roost, seemed to interest the pair as well. Sometimes, to Ruth's consternation, she figured that instead of messing about in the woods, playing in that silly den, dreaming their lives away, she knew she could have found them something more constructive to do.

Ruth stepped into the garden carrying the colander, intending to pick a few peas, "Just look at all that mess, wood everywhere." Joe smiled up at his Mother, "We're making you a new washing basket." Ruth shook her head and smiled, the boy was growing up so fast, seven years old now, it seemed no time at all since he was a baby at her breast. But here they were, the year was 1912, and here was her son and his father happily spending time together, playing about with bits of wood and chatting, seemingly not a care in the world. Ruth Ford pondered to herself, just how long would this happy state of affairs last, especially now there was talk of War?

Joe spoke up, "I'll do that Mam." Just then, a magpie, followed swiftly by another, flew onto the roof of the old shed. Reuben in excited fashion, pointed to the first bird, and turning to the boy said, "One for sorrow," Joe immediately responded with the words, "two for joy." Both smiled. Ruth, wondering what the pair could be talking about, one for sorrow, two for joy, gave a shake of her head held on to the colander and walked towards the patch of peas.

Reuben and Joe knew the significance attached to a pair of magpie. For quite a few summers now they had been playing this little game. Reuben had realised a long time ago that the magpie came every year around the same time, early summer, he had heard from Saul, the old yokel, a story told in rhyme about these birds having one partner for life, and if one died then it was 'One for sorrow.' But two together meant, 'two for joy.' Saul, had recited all the words at the time, Reuben couldn't remember the rest. It was a silly country saying, folklore. Or was there something, in the old poem? A few years down the line, these words were to be so crucial in the lives of Reuben and his son Joe.

CHAPTER 2

DIFFERENT PATHS

"What is it, my dear,; you look as though you've seen a ghost?" Ruth Ford was dishing up the evening meal of mutton stew. Joe, seated at the table, looked towards his father. Reuben, in a voice, filled with emotion said. "Wheelers Grange, its being sold. I've lost my part time job Lass. The new owners will be taking over in about a month, so old Carter informed me, reckons the new bloke will be bringing his own gardener." Reuben lowered his head, "We're sunk love; well and truly sunk. I never thought Silas Carter would give up the old Grange." Ruth placed a comforting hand on Reuben's shoulder, they had been afraid of this, rumours of Wheelers Grange changing hands, had circulated around Applebee for some time, and now it was happening,
"You'll find another job Reuben, you're a good worker. Perhaps Jethro Wickets can give you more work? There is always plenty to do on the farm at this time of year. Go and ask him love, you never know, he will be looking for someone to give a hand with the corn and now the job at Wheelers Grange has gone, Jethro will be glad to give you extra work rather than employing a stranger." Reuben giving his wife a half- hearted smile; pushed his dinner to one side and got up from the table. "I'll go and see him love, but I'm not holding out much hope, jobs aren't so plentiful at the moment."

Joe spoke up, "Ask Mr Wickets if I can have a job after school?" Reuben ruffled his son's flaxen hair. "I'll ask him Lad, but I wouldn't hold out much hope." Young Joe smiled at his father, and holding up his thumb, said, "One for sorrow, Father." Reuben gave his boy a weak smile in return, and replied, "Two for joy, son." But would that little rhyme, he and Joe had made their own, bring him any luck?

Jethro Wickets listened as Reuben explained his reason for wanting extra employment. The old farmer shook his head in disbelief, "Like you, Reuben, I thought Silas Carter would be at Wheelers Grange till he kicked the bucket. Just goes to show, nothing's a certainty, perhaps the old boy knows summat we don't? Anyway, Reuben, I can give you extra work for the harvesting, in fact Lad, I'll be glad of it. I'd rather employ a man as I can trust, than a fly be night who only wants the money. But it will only be for the harvest, then, I'm afraid it will be back to normal. Me scratting my backside off cos I can't afford to pay you anything extra and you needing more, it's a sod, but things aren't too good at the moment, what with this talk of war, and the country in such a mess."

Reuben thanked the farmer and set off for home. He had expected that response, but only working extra for the harvesting wouldn't keep the wolf from the door, and Reuben realised that if he was to keep his family well fed and clothed, then he must look for another job besides the one on Wickets farm.

Ruth listened, while her husband told her about the part time work extending only as far as the harvest. "Jethro doesn't pay much anyway love. We were able to manage, just, with my job at the farm and Wheelers Grange, but now that's gone…" Reuben shook his head. Ruth noting the anguish said. "What about trying down at the fish dock? The cart picks up from Applebee most mornings, why don't you give it a try, Its cash in hand according to Gert Filby down the road and a feed of fresh cod when the men can snaffle some." Reuben, disheartened by the outcome of his talk with Jethro Wicket's but still determined to take care of his wife and son, nodded. "I'd better go and tell Jethro my decision, give him chance to get someone else." And giving a deep sigh, "Alright Lass, I'll give the docks a go, but don't blame me when I come home stinking of rotten fish!"

One person was broken hearted at Reuben's decision to leave the farm. Grace Wickets, fully understood the situation the young man was in, but Reuben was the son she never had and, despite trying to soft soap Jethro into giving the lad more hours, her plea landed on stony ground. "I'm sorry Reuben's going Lass, but times are hard, after this damn war,talk; things will no doubt pick up. It's a pity the lad couldn't have stuck it out, and ridden the storm, but there you are. Anyway Grace, I think Reuben will rue the day he set foot on that stinking dock but we will see."

By the time Reuben had worked on Hull Dock's for a month he was a stomach churning sick of the stench. It seemed to have taken permanent residence in his nose, and blow as he might be, was unable to get rid of the smell of fish. Ruth was more than glad of the occasional crab or chunk of cod Reuben was able to pinch from the fish sheds on the dock. But she could fully understand her husband's abhorrence of the horrible stench. He had worked as a farm hand and gardener for so long, breathing in the good fresh air; and that making a living in a stinking fishy environment was going against the grain. Ruth couldn't count the times Reuben had vomited in the lav, and on occasion, in the chamber pot in the bedroom, his stomach being unable to cope with the smell since trying to make ends meet working on the docks of Hull.

So she wasn't really surprised when Reuben mentioned he had been thinking about going into the Army. "After all love, I can't go cap in hand, back to Wickets farm and expect Jethro to take me on again, can I?" Ruth understood her husband's concern, but she wasn't so sure of this new venture, Reuben would be leaving home for, God knows how long, but if that was what her husband wanted she must go along with it.

So, after much discussion, it was decided that Reuben Ford would be going into His Majesty's Army. The news that his father would be going into the armed forces was a shock to Joe. What was he going to do without his father; they had always done everything together? This, for Joe, was a black day, the first of many he would encounter during the next harrowing months.

It was June 1913, a few weeks after Joe's eighth birthday. Ruth and the boy, where standing on the platform of Hull railway station saying goodbye to a husband and father. Reuben had received his papers and would shortly be on his way to Aldershot Barracks to begin his training for the Royal Artillery. As the noisy Steam leviathan strained to pull away from the station, Reuben leaned out of the train window to give Ruth a last kiss. He put his thumb up to Joe, "One for sorrow, Son." Joe responded, tears in his eyes, "Two for joy, Father."

As the train puffed and rattled away along the tracks, Ruth and Joe watched and listened until the rhythmic sound had disappeared, leaving behind a pall of white smoke emitting from the chimney, and a wheezing, mournful, goodbye.

Ruth, stifling a tear, put a comforting arm around her weeping son's shoulder. "Come on Lad, he'll be home on leave soon, and before we know it, you will be playing with those pigeons again like you always did. And you're father promised to write, once he gets settled, so cheer up love." Ruth tried to display a confidence she didn't feel.

Welcome letters arrived from Reuben telling his loved ones that life in the army was good, keeping to himself however, the not so good bits about square bashing, tough discipline, and sleeping in hard beds in the barracks with a load of other men, most farting, some weeping for their Mam. Reuben never told Ruth about the bullying sergeants and he did come home on leave a couple of times. But things were about to change in a big way....

For on 4th August 1914, the First World War, between England, her allies, and Germany began, and unbeknown to both Ruth and Joe Ford, it was to be quite a time before either one of them would see Reuben! Many months of anxiety, heartbreak, fear and anguish, were to be experienced by the family, frantic searching would take place, how would it end?

CHAPTER 3

MY FATHER IS ALIVE

Private Reuben Ford had been sent to Salisbury Plain, after his initial training at Aldershot barracks, for further intensive instruction, where he stayed until that fateful day when war with Germany was declared. Rumours of war had been circulating for some time, and although Britain didn't have any formal alliance with France it had been decided by the powers that be, to send an expeditionary force over the channel in the event of a German attack. Herbert Asquith's Liberal Government had hesitated briefly, but when German troops invaded Belgium, whose neutrality by a treaty to which Great Britain had been one of the signatories. Britain declared war on Germany on August 4th 1914.

When the call to arms came on that fateful day, Reuben, along with countless other soldiers, was shipped across the English Channel to Calais. If they had thought the training camps were hard, then the naïve soldier was to discover a hell on earth when he reached his destination, in the living nightmare that was Ypres, Loos, or the many other battlefields of France. For many young lads it was to be where they took their final breath.

Some of the more adventurous boys tried to show bravado they didn't feel, others cried but most displayed a petrified numbness. It was at the battle of Ypres that Reuben was wounded, as were many other poor lads. Horses pulling the canvas covered ambulances, and mules over loaded with ammunition didn't fair any better, the beasts frightened out of their wits by the absolute horror they were enduring, squealed and screamed, each showing the whites of their eyes as they experienced this living hell. Reuben had asked himself, 'Why would the powers that be, think it alright to use Gods creatures in such a way?' Reuben was unable to find an answer to that particular question.

His battalion was situated at the end of the British line, and the beginning of the French line, when there was an explosion. Unfortunately for Reuben, he took the force of the shell, and was blown face down into the trench. The day was hot and oppressive. Most of the men including Reuben had stripped to the waist, trying, without much success to cool them selves down. Private Reuben Ford was almost naked now, due to the ferocity of the blast, the only clothing on his blood stained body was a one boot, and half a blood soaked trouser leg.

Reuben was floating in a pool of beautiful warm light. There was a Magpie, it was tapping at his kitchen window, Joe was calling him .He could hear his son, "Two for joy, Father, two for joy." Reuben didn't answer. Two French stretcher-bearers picked up Private Reuben Ford from where he had fallen and carried him to the French field Hospital.

Immediately after the carnage, British forward command despatched the sad news of the many losses to the war office, which duly forwarded the wretched messages.

Ruth saw the Postman at the garden gate. He walked up the path as she opened the door. "A telegram, Mrs Ford" He said. Ruth noted the air of solemnity in the eyes and voice of the elderly postman. She wondered how many of these nightmare telegrams old Sam Clifford had delivered lately, to wives and mothers of Lads being injured or slaughtered in this hellish War. Dozens upon dozens she reckoned.

Oh, Ruth knew what the telegram was, before she opened the envelope. The last letter she had received from Reuben had been weeks ago, she had been expecting bad news for some time. The newspapers had kept the reader regularly informed of the missing on the battlefields of Marne, Ypres, and many others. Ruth opened the envelope and read.... 'Dear Mrs Ford, we regret to inform you that 23797 Private Reuben Ford, is reported missing in action, any further information will be communicated to you immediately we receive it. General Arnold Baker, War office.

Ruth clutched the letter tightly in her hand. What the telegram meant, and didn't say, was that Reuben had been killed. She knew it. "Reuben! Oh my Reuben! Dear God." She felt violently sick, "Darling, my darling," She cried. "No, no, you can't be dead! Please God, don't let him be dead!" Someone was holding a bottle of smelling salts under her nose. Ruth looked up through the haze of hell, she clutched at the hand that was holding the foul smelling potion, "Father is that you?" He's dead, Reuben's dead!" Eli, taking a firm hold of his daughters hand, "Alright lass, your father's here, now come on, don't take on so. The telegram, didn't say he was dead, think of the boy love please." Ruth could think of nothing but Reuben, he was dead, somewhere on the battlefields of France......His body was lying in a stinking hole, dead.

Eli met Joe when the boy was walking the short path to Magpies Roost. "Is it true Granddad, Mam's had a letter from London?" He asked quietly. Eli nodded to the boy, "Your Mother's in the kitchen, go easy son." Joe stepped through the door, to be met with his mother cries, it wasn't chilly, but he felt something akin to cold. Ruth looked towards her son, and trying to control herself, said. "Come and sit down love." She held out the nightmare communication to her son.

Joe read the words, 'Missing in France,' the words seemed to hit him in the middle of his chest. "My Father; No! , he isn't dead Mam, he can't be, not my Father! Don't believe it Mam, it isn't true, my father isn't dead. He'll come home again, you'll see Mam." Ruth took the weeping boy into her arms, she should have realised that he was the one who would take the news of his father being missing, very badly. Ruth felt fear grip her stomach, "Come on, love, we must try to be brave."

Joe pulled away from his mothers hurting embrace and ran from the kitchen. Once in his bedroom, Joe slammed the door shut, walked across to his bed and lay spread eagled on the rough blanket and wept. His heart-wrenching sobbing could be heard downstairs. Ruth made a move to go and comfort Joe but her father took her arm. "Leave him be, Lass, let the boy cry it out."

Joe was thinking of his friend Pete Thorn. His Mam had received one of these rotten telegrams, telling them that her husband Jack was missing, presumed dead. That was a few weeks ago, and Pete's Mam had heard nothing since, so how did the blokes in the London offices know he was dead? They hadn't found his body!! Jack Thorn may still be alive, and his own Father, well, he was alive, Joe knew it; .He just knew it.

Reuben was alive alright, trouble was, he had been taken to a field hospital on the French side, and because the blast had knocked him out cold, stripping the man almost naked, there was very little on his blood soaked body, to indicate which side he belonged to - French or British! One of the reasons for this was that Reuben was fighting towards the end of the British line, and the start of the French line, when the blast came. In the bloody confusion of screaming men, body parts strewn all over the place, terrified horses and mules so traumatised by the experience of war, squealing like stuck pigs and terrified out of their minds. Reuben was found lying in the French line, beside one of the poor mangled horses, and a dead mule, which appeared to be staring up to the sky out of an empty bloody eye socket. So, Private Reuben Ford was accidentally thought to be a French casualty, for not only had he been blown further down the French side owing to the ferocity of the German shell that had landed close by, but he was covered, in his own blood, and that of the dead horse and mule.

Weeks went by without a word from the War Office. Ruth had stopped looking for old San Clifford. She reckoned the poor postman must be downhearted being asked by anxious wives and mothers, "Any news Sam?" The poor bloke seamed to take it to heart, with every sad shake of his head, when asked the question he obviously detested.

Ruth had become more and more concerned about her Mother and Father. They had taken the news about Reuben with heavy hearts. Eli was well up on the statistics of war casualties, being an avid reader of the newspapers. He, more than Kate, knew the likelihood of Reuben ever making it home, was almost nil. The old man was worried for his Daughter. Ruth seemed to be fading away before his eyes, and as for Kate, she wasn't fairing much better. Joe appeared to be the strong one, repeating over and over, that his Father was alive. Either he wouldn't accept the inevitable, that his Father was probably dead, or he felt something, deep inside that nobody else did? But his Grandson was adamant for he kept repeating, over and over, "My Father is alive, my Father is alive."

Two months after receiving the telegram from the War Office, Ruth was taken ill, Doctor's diagnosed some sort of mental breakdown. Despite Kate and Eli doing their best to take care of their daughter at home, it became too much of a burden, and besides, there was the boy to think of, he had been witness to far too much already. Ruth was taken to a sanatorium some miles away, St Cuthbert's on the outskirts of Hull. She was to be there for many months. Unfortunately for Kate, the worry of her daughter's sickness had been too much strain on her already weak heart. Eli, taking an early morning cup of tea to his wife, found Kate dead in bed.

A massive heart attack had taken Kate Jennings. Eli knew what it was, he had been expecting as much. Now as far as he could see, it was just him and Joe. How would they cope? The boy was traumatised enough at the loss of his Father, and as far as Eli was concerned, Reuben Ford was dead, and Joe's Mother being miles away at St Cuthbert's Sanatorium, just compounded the situation further and now this. Eli sat down on the horsehair sofa in the sparsely furnished room, "Oh Kate, what am I going to do without you?" He put his head in his hands and wept. "How much bloody more can I take?"

Well, it turned out that Eli Jennings was about to take on much more than he had anticipated. He had talked to young Joe, and asked him to move into the cottage with him. "We can keep each other company." He'd said to his Grandson, besides, Eli didn't feel the same any more, this wasn't home...without Kate, but the response to his suggestion had quite surprised the old man. "Why don't you come and live at Magpies Roost with me Granddad, then we will be here when Father comes home?" Eli thought on this suggestion. Why should he be surprised? Joe had been adamant all along that Reuben would come home.

Joe, at the age of nine, was older than his years. The Lad had suffered, he was still suffering, and he was as convinced as ever, that his Father would be coming home from the war and his mother would get better, and come home from the sanatorium.

So on a cool October day, 1915, Eli moved into Magpies Roost. It wasn't ideal but the old man reckoned that if staying in his own home was the best thing to keep Joe happy, then that is what he must do. He would move into Magpies Roost, and live with his grandson, it was a nice cottage and Eli quite liked the tiny bedroom where he was to sleep.

The boy was very quiet these days. The trauma of his Mother's illness and the death of his Granny had lay heavy on his heart. Keeping himself busy, by taking care of his Father's pigeons, seemed to be the only thing that brought a smile to the lads face. His Granddad was relieved that something kept the boy occupied. Eli had been at his wits end trying to pacify the lad. He had asked himself time and time again why God allowed all this misery! But he never received an answer.

There was one pigeon in particular however, by the name of Kitchener, a name given to this special bird by Joe, he had decided on the name ever since his Father had gone in the army. It must have some significance to the boy. Joe treated the pigeon more like a friend, than a bird. Reuben had told Joe to get rid of this pigeon more than once as, in his eyes, it would never be any good as it was a small and weak specimen and not worth its keep. Joe, for once, did not do his fathers bidding as he had a feeling that the bird was special.

This hadn't gone unnoticed by his Granddad. Eli had noted that this particular pigeon seemed more intelligent than the others, he had mused to himself that Kitchener seemed to understand everything the boy said to him. His feathered friend being tame enough to sit on the lad's shoulder as he whittled bits of wood in the yard at the back of the cottage.

Joe's flaxen hair was sun bleached and unkempt now. The weather had been particularly hot, baking people, and plants to a crisp. But now the winter season was beginning to rear its head, changing everything. It was too cold to sit whittling in the yard, so Eli and Joe chopped wood for the fire, in preparation for the long winter nights, and did some much needed repairs to the pigeon coop. This unfortunately was to be Eli's downfall, for as Joe and his Granddad worked on repairing the coop, the accident that was to change lives, happened.

Eli had climbed the ladder and was hammering a nail into the new door of the coop, when he hit his hand with the hammer. So hard was the blow, that Eli fell, landing with a thud on the hard ground? "Granddad, Granddad!" Joe cried. Eli lay motionless where he had fallen, one leg splayed out in an awkward position. "Please Granddad, why won't you talk to me? Don't be dead! Please, don't be dead!" On hearing the commotion through the wall, Bill Jobson, almost collided with the panic stricken Lad. "It's me Granddad Mr Jobson! I think he's dead, he won't talk to me, and he's bleeding from the head and his leg looks funny!" Joe tried to explain.

The blacksmith patted Joe on his shoulder, "Alright son, lets go and have a look." And rushed past, as soon as he got in the yard, he could see the old man was in a bad way. The head injury was very bloody, and the way Eli was lay suggested, to the blacksmith, that the old man had sustained a broken hip in the fall, he'd seen similar in a horse or two. Horses weren't people, Bill knew that, but a broken hip was a broken hip!

Pulling a grubby piece of paper and pencil from his pocket, the blacksmith scribbled a note, and giving it to the boy said. "Take this to Dr De Witt, quick as you can. I'll stay here with your Granddad, till you get back." Bill Jobson was fond of the lad, well why wouldn't he be? Joe Ford was part of his Mam, and he missed seeing Ruth's smiling face around the place.

When he arrived, Dr Samuel De Witt confirmed the Blacksmiths diagnosis, and Eli was taken to hospital. Bill Jobson had assured the doctor that he would take care of the boy for a few days, until arrangements for his care could be sorted out. But when, after two days of tears he had been unable to stop, and the boy refusing any food whatsoever, the blacksmith decided to call on Grace, at Wickets farm. He felt guilty, at his decision to give up on the boy, but quite frankly, he didn't know how to treat young un's. Joe was a nice lad, but Bill Jobson was far too busy to be bothered with looking after anybody.

Grace listened sympathetically while, Bill Jobson, told her of the dilemma.

"Do you think you could take him in Lass? God knows I've tried to care for him, but it's like flogging a dead horse, he won't eat, he just mopes about weeping, wanting to go back home all the time. Say's he must be there when his Father comes home."

Grace looked Bill Jobson firmly in the eye. "I expect you think the same as me, and the rest of Applebee, Reuben Ford is dead, like most of the other poor beggars out in that hell hole, dead as a door nail?" Bill nodded his head, "I do Lass, but young Joe won't have it, all you get is, 'My Father is alive', and nothing will convince the lad otherwise.

So it was decided that Joe Ford would stay with Grace and Jethro Wickets on the farm. It had been a shame they hadn't been able to help his Father a while back, when he had been after more work, when old Carter had laid him off at Wheelers Grange. But perhaps now they would be able, in part, to make amends by giving his Lad a home for as long as was needed.

This was to turn out harder than anyone involved could imagine. Joe Ford had always been a polite likable boy, open faced and easy to get on with, but since the turn of events had stacked against him, his Father missing in action, his Mother in a Sanatorium, his Grandmother dead, and now his Grandfather in hospital, probably for months. It was difficult to believe things could get any worse for Joe Ford, but they were about to!

Joe had been at Wickets Farm for about three weeks, in that short space of time he had run home to Magpies Roost five times, and five times Jethro had brought him back to the farm. "It's no good love we can't go on like this. I'll be worn to a frazzle running back and forth between Magpies Roost and the farm." Jethro said to Grace. Grace Wickets looked at her husband. "It's not the lads fault, Jethro, the poor little devil doesn't belong here and he knows it. Lets just give it one more try for his Father's sake, I'll have another word with him."

Grace found Joe, where she always found him, talking to his pigeon. Jethro had extended his own pigeon coop, in order to make room for the one being Joe's pet, Kitchener. The other three, that had belonged to Joe and Reuben, had gone into a pie ages ago, after having their necks pulled by the farmer, "No room for soppy sentiment." he'd said, much to the indignation of young Joe Ford, who would make sure that Kitchener didn't go the same way as the others.

So it was for this reason that every evening the boy would release Kitchener from the coop and let him go, knowing full well that the bird would fly home to Magpies Roost, thus giving him an excuse to run home, with a pretext of bringing the pigeon back. Joe knew he had to. His Father would be coming home one day and Joe must be there to meet him. He didn't care what people said about his Father being dead, he wasn't, instinct told him his Father was alive, and he, his Father, Mother and Granddad would, one day, all be back home in Magpies Roost, where they belonged.

Meanwhile, back on the front line in France, Private 23797 Reuben Ford was being cared for by hard worked French medical staff in the field hospital. To call the place a hospital was, to say the least, an over statement, for so basic were the conditions, that many of the men, despite the best being done for them, died of gangrenous open wounds, dysentery and fever, or a melange of many horrible conditions. Reuben had lain on a stinking bloody bed for two days. He hadn't stirred apart from an occasional tremble, and a shaking of his head, he was a pitiful bag of humanity.

On about the forth day Reuben could be heard mumbling incoherently, the French Doctor, who was tending his wounds, listened to what the man was trying to say. "One for, one for sorrow, Joe, there he is Joe. Sorrow, sorrow Joe." At the same time, a Magpie could be heard outside the hospital window, making its harsh chittering call. The bird seemed to be on a mission. This went on for days, the Magpie making its plaintive cry outside the hospital tent, and Reuben mumbling, every time, he heard the bird. Doctors and staff had shaken their heads, the poor man was demented, and nobody seemed able to understand his ramblings. So after tending to Reuben's physical needs, it was decided to send him to a base Hospital in Paris, where it was hoped, the soldier, whoever he was, would receive proper treatment for what ailed him. As the ambulance taking Reuben, pulled away from the field hospital, the Doctors and nurse, who had been caring for him, shook their heads and carried on tending the poor scraps of humanity who came unconscious, insane, or screaming through their doors seeking miracles.

The base hospital was on the outskirts of the City, this was a blessing in many ways, for, although Paris had taken a hammering with many fine buildings flattened, people killed, maimed or displaced, the hospital had taken little, in terms of damage or casualty. 'Big Bertha,' the notorious weapon of destruction, used by Germany, the so- called 'Big Gun,' although causing death and mayhem in Paris, had, had little impact on the hospital. In fact, from the interior, the Claude Renee Hospital was virtually unscathed.

The soldier without identity, was wheeled into the ward, he was taken to the bed nearest the nurse's station. This was usual practice for the newest poorly patients who arrived at the Claude Renee Hospital.

Reuben was still falling in and out of consciousness. He had taken a terrible battering, and although the bruising, which was pretty much all over his body, was beginning to fade, and bones were knitting together, the soldiers mind was in turmoil. Where was he? Who were all these strangers? And, the unanswered question, where was Joe? Who was he anyway? Why were these people speaking French, and why couldn't he sit up? Reuben felt that if he didn't get out of this prone position, he would go mad, or was he mad already? He couldn't breathe, and pain was everywhere, Reuben had screamed silently to God, but it seemed God hadn't answered.

The journey from the field hospital had been a hard one. The two horses that had pulled the Ambulance had been terrified, being able to sense the horror no doubt, for although the vehicle had only skirted the City of Paris, there was plenty of evidence of the carnage this terrible war was causing. The Ambulance had passed shelled and burnt out buildings. Scarecrow hollow eyed people, wandering about among the ruins, dead bodies, in a state of rigor mortis, one pointing a decaying hand to the sky, as if pleading with God for release, a dead woman holding a baby. There was a mangled cat, lying dead amongst the rubble, and bizarrely, a huge rat was making a meal of the carcass, much to the horror of both Ambulance men who had watched this grotesque scene, one of whom, sickened by the whole affair, vomited where he sat

When Reuben Ford had been a patient in the Claude Renee Hospital for six days, it seemed God had heard his cries. He was dreaming once more, the same dream as always, he was at home, and in the kitchen of Magpies Roost, it was early summer, he and Joe were standing by the window when a Magpie flew down, landing on the roof of the shed. "One for sorrow Joe, one for sorrow." called Reuben, and as always, in the dream, a second Magpie followed the first, only for Joe to answer, "Two for joy Father. Two for joy.. Reuben, distraught, began to weep. He was recalling in his mind, happier days. He had a wife and Son, he lived at Magpies Roost, he reared pigeons. he worked the land. He wanted to go home! In his troubled mind Reuben prayed, or did he, in reality, scream out loud? "Dear God, help me!"

Suddenly from the opposite side of the hospital a man shouted out, "Un, de, tristesse,   un de tristesse." Reuben, who had picked up a few words of French, heard the voice and he recognised the French translation, these few words seemed to unlock the door to Reuben's troubled mind. Whoever the soldier was, British or French, the man had done Reuben a huge favour, perhaps it was a cry of frustration from a patient who was sick or hearing the mad mans blathering? Well whatever the reason, something had done the trick. Quick as a flash, Reuben was wide-awake, "One for sorrow Joe,; one for sorrow."

Once it had been established that Private Reuben Ford had been taken to the wrong hospital, he was very soon transported to the British field hospital on the outskirts of Lille, where he was to stay for quite a time. His mind was to remain troubled for a long time, unable to grasp what was real and what was fantasy. The nightmares were to continue well into the future, he would experience depression at its worst, and elation at its best.

Word had been sent to Mrs Ruth Ford, at the Sanatorium, when the Soldier had been found, but unfortunately because of some blunder, the letter never arrived. Ruth was to remain, in ignorance of the fact that Reuben was alive, for some time to come. Unfortunately, this wasn't an isolated case. A good many found themselves in a similar boat. But happily in Mr& Mrs Ford's case, fortune was to shine on them in a most unusual way.   Reuben, because of his wounds, would never see active service again, but he was to experience much heartache, before God, in his wisdom, decided enough was enough.

Meanwhile, back on Wicket's Farm, things were going from bad to worse. Grace mopped her brow, "I can't stand much more of this, Jethro, the lad will have to go. This, back and forth from Magpies Roost, will finish me, and I can't see you putting up with much more." Jethro nodded his head. They both liked the boy, but him running back home, all the time, was becoming very wearing. Work was beginning to suffer. Grace and Jethro couldn't let this state of affairs go on any longer. "We need to get in touch with the authorities," said Jethro, "I feel sorry for the boy, Lass, but we can't go on like this. God only knows when his Mother will be fit to take care of him, if ever, and Reuben, what of him, dead I shouldn't wonder? Oh, I know young Joe believes his Father is still alive, but I don't Grace, and that's the truth. The man's rotted away in some far flung hole in the ground."

CHAPTER 4

GRIMTHORPE HALL

"Are you sure Joe will be alright Jethro? You know the state of the Lad's mind just lately. It's a long way for him to travel, are you sure we're doing the right thing, that school didn't look very Christian to me?" Grace asked her husband. "Well it's a children's home, run by the church, Grace, so it should be alright. Anyway love, the authorities thought it was the right thing to do. The boy needs discipline, and I feel sure he will get just that at Grimthorpe Hall. He won't be able to go running back to Magpies Roost every five minutes. And after all, we can't be expected to look after Joe Ford forever." Grace gave Jethro a week smile, "I hope your right."

Joe had got wind of the situation, and he didn't like it. Why couldn't anyone see that he needed to be at Magpies Roost for when his Father came back home, and he would be coming home, just as soon as he could. So was his Mother and Granddad, when they were well enough, and it was up to him to make sure he was at home when they arrived.

It had been weeks, long lonely weeks, and now Mr& Mrs Wickets were sending him to a school, miles away, and Joe wasn't going without a fight. He had been making plans for himself and Kitchener. Each time during these last few days he had gone to Magpies Roost, he had taken provisions, a chunk of cheese here, a few apples there, a thick slice of cured bacon wrapped in a muslin cloth, this was easy, the smoke house was right next to his room, it had been simple to take a sharp knife and cut a thick rasher of bacon. His canvas bag was full of enough food to feed Kitchener and himself for some time to come, wherever he went, so did his pigeon. There was wooden shutter in his room on the farm, covering a chute leading to the hayloft. The door had been nailed up when it had been decided to turn the space into a bedroom for the lad. Joe knew that when the time came, he would be able to make use of the chute, it wouldn't be difficult to remove the nails in the old door, he would bide his time, after all, if bails of hay could fit into the chute, so could he. Once in the hayloft, he and Kitchener would be able to make their escape, run back to Magpies Roost and barricade themselves in. Joe Ford wasn't going to Grimthorpe Hall.

A wooden box, with holes punched in the lid, had already been placed into the tunnel behind the door. Joe had manoeuvred a small plank of wood into the top of the chute, thus preventing the box hurtling into the hay loft, this box was to be the means by which he could carry Kitchener when he left the farm and went back home for good. Joe had noted the policeman and a fat, well-dressed bloke, talking to Mr Wickets and the tear-stained face of the farmers' wife. Furtive looks and anxious voices told the boy to make haste, and get away from Wickets Farm, as soon as he could.

He was just emerging from the bottom of the chute, when he felt something grip his ankle, it was too dark to make out who it was. Then he heard the voice of Mr Wickets. "Come on lad, where do you think your going this time?" Joe struggled, trying to free his leg, and at the same time keep tight hold of Kitchener in the wooden box. Joe kicked out, he felt panic rising, his heart was beating fast. "Leave me alone! I'm not going to that place! You can't make me!" He looked pleadingly across at Mrs Wickets who was stood weeping nearby, with a handkerchief to her eyes. She shook her head and scurried into the farmhouse.

"Let me go home to Magpies Roost, please, Mr Wickets! I've got to be there for my Father, please Mr Wickets!" Joe could feel the choking tears in the back of his throat, "Let me go home, I will be alright, I've got food there." Then in beaten defiance, "You just wait till my Father comes home. He'll get you!" But despite all Joe's tears and pleading, he was soon in the carriage and on his way to Grimthorpe Hall.

It was quite dark, six fifteen in the evening. The snow that had been threatening all day had arrived about two hours earlier. As the horses trotted along the track made more dangerous by the unexpected snowfall. Hooves and cartwheels slipped in the deep furrows made by carts and horses hooves that had previously made their way along this treacherous track. The heavy, laboured breathing of the horses could be heard as they tried to overcome the tricky conditions, snorts of smoky white breath evident against the moonlight, as the poor beasts tried to keep a firm foothold. Sometimes a pitiful whinny could be heard as a hoof slipped, off balancing the frightened animal, only to be followed by a loud, "Get up there! Trot on!" and the crack of a whip.

Once out into the countryside, conditions were better, horses were able, in part, to trot on virgin snow, the white blanket affording a little more light. Joe carefully opened the lid of the wooden box that was to be Kitchener's home for the foreseeable future. He didn't know what he was going to do, or where he would be living, but he and Kitchener had made it so far. Joe peered into the homemade box, he was just able to put his finger in and locate the bird's head. Kitchener responded with a little cooing sound, Joe heaved a sigh of relief. They weren't alone in the carriage, but the old man opposite, had been asleep for most of the time. Joe thought his fellow passenger smelled funny, sort of sickly sweet, and sweaty. Anyway, he had shown little or no interest, in the boy or his box, much to Joe's relief.

Joe felt into his jacket pocket and pulled out a piece of stale bread, he offered it to the
Pigeon, who gobbled it ravenously. The old man was still sleeping. Joe felt outside the carriage door, and scooped up a

handful of snow, after taking a few welcome licks himself, he offered a little to Kitchener.

After what seemed ages, the horses trotted to a stop. Snorting and whinnying, their heads nodding up and down, as if trying to cool the sweat that was steaming from their tired bodies. The door of the carriage was flung open. A man with a lantern spoke to him, "You Joe Ford?" Joe picked up his meagre belongings and answered the man. "Yes sir." "Follow me then." Joe followed the man, as requested. They walked across what appeared to Joe, to be a dimly lit courtyard, situated in front of a large imposing building. As they approached the large porch, a boy, about Joe's age, opened the door. He was much heavier in build. What happened next was to give Joe Ford an insight into what to expect, from now on, at the hands of this boy. "Alright Perks, you can leave the new boy with me." Mr Perks, Joe now knew the name of the man who had met him, grunted his answer. "Your Father told me to see to the new Lad, Mr Horace." It struck Joe that Mr Perks didn't much care for the boy at the door. The fat boy reared up at Mr Perks, "I said, I will look after this one, now get on your way, Perks." Then turning to face Joe , said. "Come on then boy don't just stand there." Joe tucked the box holding Kitchener carefully under his jacket, picked up his bag and followed the fat boy.

"My name is Horace Sourby. My father is the Headmaster of Grimthorpe Hall, so you'd better mind me." Joe had already taken the measure of the other boy, and he didn't like what he saw. Horace Sourby was fat as pudding. Joe noticed as he walked behind the boy, that his legs were so large they seemed to rub together, and his bum was enormous, wobbling in rhythm with each step. The boy's hair was ginger, his eyes piggy looking. In fact Horace Sourby looked what he was, horrible. The other thing to hit Joe was the smell in this building, carbolic soap, old books and stale broth. The place seemed very old and imposing. Joe clutched at the box inside his jacket.

Just then, there was a commotion, as Mr Perks confronted the fat boy. "I can hear you Sourby; , the boy doesn't have to, 'mind you,' as you put it. Just because your Father is Head Master of Grimthorpe Hall, doesn't give you the right to ride roughshod over every new boy "Now out of my way!" With that the Headmasters son stumbled as Mr Perks pushed him hard against the wall. "My Father will hear of this, Perks, and you will be out of a job!" Then he turned red faced to Joe, "You'd better watch out from now on." The porter turned to Joe, "Come on lad, take no notice of the bloody coward, but watch him mind, he's a bad 'un!" Joe thought it would be a very good idea to heed the warning he had been given.

He was escorted down a long, dark corridor, which opened into a cold dank cobble floored washroom, where awaited the Matron of Grimthorpe Hall, Miss Daphne Crabtree. The woman was in her late thirties, rather austere looking, with starched uniform and starched features. So when the smile came, it quite surprised the Lad. "Get out of those clothes and into the bath." Joe, who was still shaken by what he had just witnessed, and keeping tight hold of the box, looked up at the woman. She nodded, as if understanding how he was feeling. The Matron held her hands out for the box, at the same time, dismissing Horace Sourby. "You can go now, close the door on your way out." The hard tone of the dismissal didn't go unnoticed by Joe. He handed his box to Miss Crabtree. "Now; into the bath with you." She said. Joe shivering, and naked, did as he was asked. The water was cloudy and smelled odd. Just then the door opened and in came the man who had met him when he'd arrived earlier.

"Give the boy a good delousing, Perks," said the Matron, " make sure you wash his hair, take his clothes down to the laundry, anything too far gone, burn, the rest can be washed, and collect his uniform on the way back." Mr Perks, suitably subservient replied, "Yes Matron." "Then Perks," she said, "take the boy to the kitchen, I expect cook will find him something to eat, after that, I want you to make sure he goes to his room."

Joe, deloused, even though he hadn't needed the treatment, got out of the bath. He dried himself on the rough towel, put on the uncomfortable robe provided and picked up his box from the floor where the matron had put it. He then followed Mr Perks out of the washhouse.

They arrived at the kitchen. Joe was overawed at its size and he gazed about him. White tiles from floor to ceiling covered the walls. A giant cooker seemed to take up most of the far wall opposite the door. There was a large deep sink, which appeared to be full of pots. A large woman in a white and green uniform came towards Mr Perks and Joe.
"Evening Nellie, got a bite to eat, for this new un?" Mr Perks asked her. The cook gave a tired smile to Mr Perks, and looking towards Joe, "Aye' come on Lad, you just arrived? Sit thee down, and I'll fetch thee a bite of summit." Joe thanked the nice woman and sat down at the table, and tried to check on Kitchener, who by now was becoming a bit of a worry. He must get the bird out of the box soon! Joe wasn't to know that further down the line Nellie Plumly, the cook, was to be an ally and a friend.

After a meal of bread, cheese, some of which Joe managed to stuff into his pocket, intending to give some to Kitchener, and a mug of milk, he was escorted along a corridor to a small square room. Joe was later to learn this cell like place was called the 'holding room,' it was where the new boys were put until they had been assessed as to their schooling and background. This couldn't be better, as far as Joe Ford was concerned, he didn't intend staying at Grimthorpe Hall for very long.

Once he was inside the small room, and Mr Perks had gone, Joe opened the box, there wasn't any movement. The lad felt inside, Kitchener was cold to the touch, "Don't be dead, please, don't be dead." Joe gently lifted the bird out of the 'prison' and laid him on the bed, and then out of his pocket he took a morsel of bread. "Come on Kitchener, wake up. We're here now, but not for long, I'll take you back to Magpies Roost as soon as I can, but for now we must be careful." Joe looked apprehensively around him. The room was small and contained a bed, a dresser that had seen better days, a small table and chair. There was a lit candle on the table, beside a Bible, and a crucifix on the wall. There was a tiny leaded light window with a stiff catch.

Just then Kitchener stirred and lifted his head. Joe relieved, stroked the bird's neck.
"Good boy Kitchener, good boy." Joe went over to the window and looked out, against the full moon he could see snow falling. He opened the stiff window, and putting his arm outside, he gathered a handful of soft snow, which soon turned to liquid in the warmth of his hand, he walked back to the bed and gently offered the water to Kitchener. At the same time he put a drop on the bird's head, after a while Joe was relieved to see an improvement in the bird's demeanour.

Joe sat down on the bed. On investigation he found that apart from what seemed to be the only blanket, there was a pair of rough sheets and a hard pillow. It didn't matter much, he didn't intend staying long at Grimthorpe Hall, he had to get back to Magpies Roost as quickly as he could. Unfortunately, however, Joe Ford would be a guest of the Hall for a while yet and a target for his tormentor… Horace Sourby.

When he had been there for a couple of days, and Kitchener was fully recovered, Joe decided to do a little investigating when he could. It wasn't going to be easy, ever since the contretemps with Horace Sourby on that first day, tension between the boys had become volatile. A menial, namely the porter, had showed up Horace and he wasn't going to let Perks or Joe get away with that. So Joe had to be on his guard at all times. But he wasn't going to stay here any longer than he had to, his Father was coming home soon, and he had to be there when he arrived.

Joe had discovered that he was able to squeeze through the tiny window in his room. The fact that he had lost a little weight recently was helping him. He had managed to climb out of the window on two occasions. The first time enabled the lad to familiarise himself with the surroundings, the second, he was able to creep to the kitchen and take some food, for the escape he was about to make.

Joe didn't know how much longer he would be in this holding room, so he didn't want to take too much longer, preparing for his journey home. He would go tonight. It was as good a time as any. He had managed to assemble quite a few supplies, namely a meat pie and a chunk of fruit cake from the larder. .He could have pinched a blancmange, except it would be difficult to carry in his canvas bag. He had taken a few oats from the sack in the kitchen, he must make sure of some food for Kitchener, the poor bird must be going crazy from being confined to this small room, but for the time being, the bird would be put back in his prison.

"Come on boy, its time to go." Joe carefully placed Kitchener into the box, tucked him under his arm, put the strap of the canvas bag over his shoulder, and climbed onto the window sill. It was dark, very dark, but Joe had practised this for quite a while, he knew just where he was, and which way to go to make his escape.

He was on the ground. All was quiet, except for the hooting of an owl nearby. The night was cold, Joe shivered, he was glad he had managed to wear two nightshirts and a shirt under his jacket. His trousers felt a little tight, but at least with the shirts tucked inside they afforded him some warmth, and the boots supplied by the school, although heavy and stiff would probably last him a life time, Joe gave a wry smile at this thought.

The boy also realised he wouldn't be able to escape through the gates, the wrought iron contraption was so heavily locked and bolted that it would be impossible. However an earlier inspection had revealed a large hole to the right of the gate, probable made by a fox. As he crept towards it, Joe thought he heard a noise, he held his breath, and prayed that Kitchener would keep quiet also. He heard another rustling sound and he kept still as death. After what seemed an eternity, Joe moved his position, all was quiet perhaps he had been mistaken?

As he lay quiet, hardly daring to breath, Joe wondered how all this had happened. What with his Mother in a sanatorium, his Granddad in hospital and his Granny dead, and finally his Father missing in France. Why was life so cruel? He wanted his Father. Tears began to mist his eyes, "Father, oh' Father, where are you?" This was his silent cry, and as if in a dream he thought he heard, "One for sorrow Joe, one for sorrow." Joe wiped his eyes with the cuff of his jacket. "Two for joy Father, two for joy." he whispered.

It would be a long time before Joe heard the Magpie's chittering call, but he would hear it again.

He had left Grimthorpe Hall behind an hour ago. Joe reckoned it must be about eleven thirty in the evening. The streets were quiet, apart from an occasional dog, and the tramp he had just seen, there was nobody about. Joe reckoned that, if his timing was correct, he should reach Magpies Roost before midnight. He decided to let Kitchener out of the box, the bird would be more than relieved to make his own way home to Magpies Roost. Joe opened the box but he couldn't detect any movement from inside. Then, all of a sudden, as if alarmed, Kitchener made a tiny squawk, and lifted his head. The next second, he was out of his confined space, and flying to the nearest tree. "Go home Kitchener, go home, I will follow you." Joe called out.

Just then, there was a scuffle behind Joe, and an angry voice shouted. "Oh no you won't boy" Joe, alarmed by the noise, turned round to be confronted by Mr Jake Sourby, Headmaster of Grimthorpe Hall, and Mr Perks.

Mr Sourby grabbed the shoulder of the frightened lad. "My son Horace was right about you. Say goodbye to that blasted bird and get into the carriage. You won't be going home for a long while yet."

The angry Headmaster unceremoniously threw Joe into the carriage. Mr Perks followed in silence, and sat down opposite Joe. If the lad could have described the look on the porters face each time he glanced towards his employer, it would have said hatred, it portrayed, pure hatred for Mr Sourby. Joe felt sick. He had come so close to escape, he sat feeling deflated. How had Mr Sourby found out? He'd been so careful, and what of Kitchener, the pigeon was all alone now, this was a nightmare, a terrible nightmare!

The horses pulled up in the courtyard of Grimthorpe Hall, the poor beasts had been made to race home, the whip could be heard cracking down on their rumps at regular intervals. Joe noticed Mr Perks clench his fist more than once, the man was fond of the animals, and it was obvious he didn't like the ill treatment, being dished out to them.

"Get him to the dormitory Perks. I'll deal with the ungrateful young bugger in the morning." shouted Mr Sourby. Mr Perks doffed his cap at Mr Sourby, more in insolence than respect, and lead the boy away. Joe had met the Headmaster, soon after he arrived at the Hall, his instincts had told him to be aware of this man. He was fat like his son Horace and he had a cruel look about him. The ginger hair was even more carroty than Horace's and he had a greasy looking moustache, as if he dipped it in his soup when he was eating. Joe had a feeling that this man didn't like him.

"Come on Lad, let's get you to bed." said Mr Perks. "Why did you run off?" You should have known you wouldn't get away with it. Other's have tried afore, without success." Joe gave the porter a look that said, ' I can't stay here.' "Please Mr Perks, help me to get away." He cried, "I must go home to Magpies Roost, my Father is missing in France, he was fighting in the war. People say he's dead, but he isn't Mr Perks, he isn't! I know he will come home, so will Mam, when she's better. And Kitchener, what about Kitchener, Mr Perks? He flew home, just before Mr Sourby caught me, he won't manage on his own, how will he survive?"

Joe must have forgotten the stash of food he had been able to take to Magpies Roost when he was planning his escape from Wickets Farm. There was sure to be an apple or two, probably mouldy by now, and some stale bread, unless a mouse or a rat had made a meal of the bounty he had managed to smuggle to the house. The lad need not have worried, pigeons are survivors, and Kitchener was no exception to this fact. He'd made it home. Pigeons don't normally fly at night, so when the bird had been set free unexpectedly, on that fateful night, he had stayed in the tree he had flown to when Joe had released him. Making his way in the morning to Magpies Roost, where he found enough food to keep him going for a while. What a pity Joe couldn't have known this. He would however, learn something that was to convince the lad that miracles do happen, if you believe in them, and Joe Ford most certainly did.

Joe followed the porter as he escorted him to a large dormitory. On each side of the long room there was a row of beds, each covered in a dark grey blanket. Joe reckoned there must be thirty, most seemed to be occupied, a smell of urine hit the back of the lads throat, and from somewhere further down the dormitory, weeping could be heard. Behind each bed there was a window, large and devoid of curtains.

Mr Perks stopped at the bottom of the third bed on the left. "This must be yours, it's the only one that doesn't have any belongings on the locker. Get out of your clothes and into your nightshirt and try to get some sleep. I'll see you in a couple of hours as its almost five o'clock now."

Joe did as he was asked, but he couldn't sleep, he hated this place, it was all strange to him. He could hear boys snoring, passing wind, or crying for their mothers, the smell of sweaty feet and farting permeated the room. He must have fallen asleep because someone was shaking him and speaking with a menacing attitude. "Get up Ford, Father wants to see you after breakfast." Joe was looking up at the bloated smirking face of Horace Sourby. He struggled to sit up, another shake from his tormentor, "you're sitting by me, in the dining hall, come on Ford."
Joe gave the fat boy a look of contempt. "Leave me alone Sourby, I've done nothing to you."

Just then, from the next bed., "I've warned you affore, Sourby, about battering the new boys. You put the last one in hospital, now leave Joe alone or you will get your head punched and for you're information, Joe can sit by me at breakfast! Now bugger off!" Joe looked across to the boy who was defending him it was the supposed bully Jack Simms! Joe had seen the boy before, and heard about some of his antics, but he hadn't spoken to him, in fact, while he had been in the holding room, he hadn't seen much of the other boys at all. "Come on Joe," Jack said, "just leave fat guts to me!"

Horace Sourby had a look on his face that resembled a smashed peach, "Just you wait till I tell my Father about you two!" He slavered, "He'll have you both skinned alive!" And with that, Sourby wobbled off towards the dining room, teeth clenched together and spluttering obscenities.

Well, it wasn't quite like that, but both boys were given a few hefty whacks with the birch. Sourby Senior, apparently enjoying the sound, as birch, landed on bare bottom.
This act of cruelty, doled out by Sourby, was to cement a friendship between Jack Simms and Joe Ford, a friendship that would last a lifetime.

After assembly, followed by morning prayers and a stirring hymn, the boys walked out of the main Hall and into the dining room. There were three long rows of tables, each with benches either side reaching from the entrance to the far end of the room where there was an elevated platform. This was used as a stage for pupils who were performing one of the plays they had learned in drama and music class, Hamlet or Othello, being chosen as the more masculine opera's performed by boys, who were that way inclined. Joe showed little or no interest in this sort of activity, he much preferred fishing, whittling wood or taking care of Kitchener. Joe heaved a sigh, where was his pigeon now?

At meal times, the staff of Grimthorpe Hall,sat in the elevated position of the stage. They had a good view of the boys down below, eating their meagre stodge while they, the staff tucked into succulent delights from the fat of the land.

Jack Simms and Joe Ford walked into the dining hall together, they each took a tray and waited in the snaking line of hungry boys making their way to the counter, where they would be given breakfast of thick porridge. The sort Joe's Father would say was thick enough to sole your boots. This lumpy offering was followed by a mug of stewed tea.

The thought of thick porridge and Reuben's comments brought the lad once more to thinking of his Father, not that he was ever far from the lad's thoughts. Neither were the rest of his family and Kitchener. What of poor Kitchener? Would he ever see his pal again?

Jack Simms gave Joe a nudge with his elbow. "What are you dreaming about, you look miles away?" Joe put the tray down on the table and shuffled along the bench.
Jack followed. They sat down and began to eat the stodge. "I was just thinking about my Father, and the rest of my family, and my pigeon Kitchener, and wondering where he is." "Didn't know you had any family, or a pigeon." said Jack. Then he added in a matter of fact way. "My Father buggered off just after I was born. Good riddance to bad rubbish I say. And as for pigeons, they can take care of themselves, so don't worry about your bird."

Joe looked at his new friend. He wasn't a bad looking lad, but it was obvious by his demeanour that Jack Simms had seen the harder side of life. Joe reckoned the lad would be about the same age as himself, give or take a few months, he wasn't as tall rather on the thin side, dark unruly hair and blue eyes. Joe liked him, he was rough and ready but Joe knew he and Jack were going to be true and lasting friends.

"Is that why you're in this place Jack?" Joe asked, "You don't have anyone?" Jack Simms smiled, "My Mother died when she was having me, and I never knew my Father, he obviously didn't want me. An old aunty looked after me for a while she was strict but nice. Then, when she died, I ended up here that was a long time ago. I've lived at Grimthorpe for three years. Its not so bad, some of um you have to watch

45

mind, Sourby and his fat son to name two, Mr Gordon, the House Master is kind, you won't have seen him yet though, he's away on holiday. Probably glad of the rest, old Sourby treats him like a slave, don't know how he puts up with it." "You seem to know a lot Jack." Jack Simms gave Joe a shrewd look. "It pays to keep on top of things in this place," he said, "especially with people like Mr Sourby and horrible Horace. Watch them Joe, you need eyes in your arse to keep ahead of that pair of rogues!"

The boys hurried down the corridor to their classroom, chatting as they went, the first lesson was arithmetic. Jack Simms hated it, especially as the Headmaster took this class. The man seemed to relish in making Jack squirm when he asked him a question that he knew the boy didn't have the answer to.

There was one member of staff however, who knew all about the treatment doled out by Mr Sourby on any boy he took a dislike to, or indeed any member of staff who didn't go along with the headmaster's warped ideas. This fact troubled Mr Gordon it always had done ever since he had started work at Grimthorpe Hall. But as his position was only that of Housemaster, he had little or no influence as to what went on within its walls. But Mr Andrew Gordon Housemaster was soon to put the cat amongst the pigeons, in defence of Joe Ford.

It was January 1916. If Christmas had been celebrated at Grimthorpe Hall, there had been very little sign of any festivity to mark the event, despite the home supposedly being run by the church. Joe recalled a few carols, and a few sprigs of holly hung in the big hall. He remembered the aroma of roast chicken wafting about the place, it had reminded him of home, but none of the boys tasted any chicken. Joe had been a guest of Grimthorpe Hall for about two months, and he didn't like the place anymore now than he had done on that first day.

One for Sorrow Two for Joy

The boys had discussed what their lives had been like before they came into Grimthorpe Hall. Jack was unable to remember much of what his life had been before this place. He was ten years old now, almost the same age as Joe. He had lived here since he was three, years old so really, the children's home was all he knew.

Joe was happy to call Jack Simms his friend the boy seemed fearless. He had shown much interest in the story Joe told him about his family, and seemed genuinely concerned about the fate of Mr & Mrs Ford, the rest of Joe's family, and of course Kitchener.

Since Joe had told him about the pigeon, and how much he cared for the bird, the boys had been saving a piece of bread or any scrap of food they could sneak, from their meagre meals. This was fed to the hungry pigeons that lived around Grimthorpe Hall. Their task was made easy as both boys worked on the gardens at the home, and it was on the vegetable patch where the pigeons congregated, when they visited, much to the dismay of Mr Sourby. The Headmaster classed all birds as vermin and would shoot the lot if he could. Jack Simms watched as his friend talked to the skinny pigeons, perhaps Joe was thinking of his own pigeon, and feeding the feral birds helped his pal.

The two boys reached the classroom at the same time as Horace Sourby. The boy's bulk taking up most of the doorway; as he walked through into the classroom,
"Come on, you two, you'd better get to your desk's at once, my Father will be here shortly." He stood back in mock politeness, as if allowing them to go before him, both boys stepped forward. Joe felt a sharp pain at the back of his head as the fist made contact. "I warned you Ford!" Joe, dazed with pain and shock, stumbled and fell on the floor in front of Sourby. There was silence for a second, then an outcry from pupils and staff who had seen the assault on the boy. Mr

Andrew Gordon, Housemaster, appalled at what he had just witnessed, hurried towards the injured boy.

Joe, as white as driven snow, lay motionless at his attacker's feet. Jack, kneeling at his friend's side, looked up towards Mr Gordon, "He's done for him Sir, Horace Sourby as done for Joe!" With that, in blind rage, Jack Simms hit out at the Headmaster's son, punching and kicking the fat bully! "You sod! You bloody swine, you've killed Joe!"
"Calm down Lad." Andrew Gordon taking control of the situation, .said ."Ford will be alright."   Jack Simms, seething with anger towards Sourby, glanced at the Housemaster. "The blow knocked him out lad, but he's breathing." Mr Gordon looked at Horace Sourby in disgust. "You'll pay for this boy, plenty of people witnessed what you did. You won't get away with it this time!"

Mr Sourby senior had to put on a show of punishing his son, but nobody believed that the belting Horace had received fitted the crime. Rather that the belt had driven more evil into the boy, than out of him. From that day on, Horace Sourby was on the warpath even more for Joe Ford and Jack Simms. He didn't take a beating for anyone so that pair had better watch out from now on!

It was in early march that Joe had some good news of his Granddad. Apparently Eli Jennings was making good progress, he couldn't walk yet, but the signs of recovery were beginning to look promising. He was eating better and looking less like a scarecrow as the weeks went by. But Eli was worried about the boy. He shouldn't be in the children's home. He'd heard talk about Grimthorpe Hall and the goings on there, and the thought of Joe being an inmate bothered the old man. When Bill Jobson had come to see him and told what had happened to Joe he was livid. It was unavoidable, Eli accepted this, but the boy should be with the Wickets, why couldn't they have persevered with the lad? Eli gave a sigh, and thought Shame on the pair of um. They knew the terrible situation, Reuben missing somewhere in France, Ruth in a sanatorium, and he himself knocked up in hospital. People were bloody callous, and them the ones supposed to care? Eli would visit his daughter and Joe just as soon as he was able. He could ask the blacksmith to take him in his horse and trap.

Joe passed on the good news to his pal. Jack was pleased, but did this good news for Joe, mean he would one day be loosing his friend? The nights that had for so long been dark, were beginning to draw out, it was light now at six thirty morning and evening, in a couple of days they would be into April.

Work on the gardens was as hard as ever. A pile of horse manure had been delivered and the boys were busy muck spreading among the plants. Suddenly, there was a whoosh of wings as the pigeons landed. This was their patch, they'd got used to being fed by the boys. What happened next was to surprise Joe. Amongst the flock there was a familiar looking pigeon. The bird was scraggy and thin, but, it was' Kitchener! Joe, hardly able to contain himself said "Kitchener! ! Jack its Kitchener! He's found me!"

It seemed Kitchener had gone back home, but because pickings were small at Magpies Roost, he had joined with the group of feral pigeons who happened to be the ones who visited Grimthorpe Hall. So in fact, Kitchener hadn't found Joe, it was just that the bird had tagged onto a group of wild pigeon, which knew where to find a meal. Did fate have a hand in the miracle? Joe Ford certainly thought so. For it was obvious that the pigeon knew Joe. Kitchener was to be seen more and more around Grimthorpe Hall, and because of this, Joe was becoming concerned for his bird's safety.

By this time most of the boys were aware that the pigeon belonged to Joe Ford. It had become pretty obvious, as the bird was always hanging around the lad when he was working in the garden. It had also been seen on the windowsill of the dormitory, and was becoming a source of excitement for the inmates of Grimthorpe Hall.

Well, that was all except the Headmaster, Sourby, and of course his horrible son. To Sourby, the pigeon was vermin, and there was no place for it at Grimthorpe Hall. Little did he know that the boys had taken such a shine to the bird, that it had been living in the dormitory for quite a while now, being cared for by all the boys, who thought the deception a game, getting one over Sourby and Horace and they were all for that.

It had been difficult getting Kitchener into the dormitory, needing all the skill and ingenuity the boys could muster. The sleeping quarters were situated on the first floor,
directly above Sourby's office and living accommodation. And considering there was a drainpipe, and a balcony with a balustrade which led into the dormitory and the office was at the end of the building, then this would be the best way in.

It had been decided that distraction tactics would be used in order to pull off the deception. So the boys got their heads together, and between them came up with a plan. Alfred Pitcher and Bill Dickens would start a fight in the middle of the night, the rest of the boys aiding and abetting so loudly that the whole of Grimthorpe would be in uproar. Then in the melee, Frank Bilbo, wiry and nimble, who could climb like a monkey, would shin up the drainpipe with Kitchener, and wait on the balcony until all was quiet, then into the dormitory, through a window that had been left open.
Everything went to plan at first and the supposed fight could definitely be heard all over Grimthorpe Hall. Boys yelling and squealing, bumping and banging as furniture was toppled about to add to the din. Frank Bilbo had managed to reach the balcony, while a disgruntled Headmaster, clad only in a stripped nightshirt dashed about like a scalded cat, "What the

hell is going on here? Just you wait. I'll get you, you buggers!" Luckily for Bilbo, the boy managed to shin the drainpipe before Sourby had wiped the sleep from his piggy eyes. He placed the box holding Kitchener, under Joe Ford's bed, the boys, dishevelled and sweaty, were all tucked up and feigning sleep, the dormitory looked like a war zone.

The door was flung open! The Headmaster; nightshirt clad, stood seething with rage .He shouted at the top of his voice.
"Out of bed at once" Now who's idea was this?" His piggy eyes alighted on Alfred Pitcher and the black eye, "Anything to say boy? You'd better have a good excuse this time." His eyes scanned the rest of the boys, most were bruise free, except for Frank Bilbo, who had a pair of bloody shins and a cut head. Sourby glared at his two victims, "Get to my office the pair of you, The rest can clean this dormitory, and don't expect any breakfast this morning!" With that he slammed out.

The hiding that was given to Alfred Pitcher and Frank Bilbo was of Sourby's usual standard, brutal and cruel. Every lash enjoyed by the evil so and so. Once again, bruised bottoms and dignity were given salve, Matron Crabtree noting the extent of the humiliation, both physical, and mental, wondered again, how Sourby could do this to the boys in his charge.

Bill Dickens, who had blacked Pitchers eye, was relieved he had been spared a hiding, but never the less, vowed to pay Sourby back, one way or another, for all his cruelty.

Kitchener was made welcome in the dormitory by all the boys, he was well fed, as all the lads did their best to bring a morsel of food, sneaked from their meagre diet, be it a chunk of dry bread, oat biscuit or a handful of thick porridge stuffed into a piece of rag. All the talk was of Kitchener and his welfare, he was allowed to fly free in the dormitory when the door was locked at night he was even trusted on the windowsill. Sometimes going off for a time, but always coming back, for as the saying goes, Kitchener knew by now, which side his bread was buttered. Joe was relieved to have his pal with him and happy that the other boys were interested in Kitchener. The bird was clever, extraordinary some would say, and he was to prove his worth in ways that would astound.

Unfortunately however, as a group of the boys walked to class from the dormitory, the Headmaster overheard their conversation. Reared up in anger at Joe Ford, who was singing the praises of Kitchener. "What the blazes do you know about Kitchener, Ford?" Joe quick off the mark, answered. "Field Marshall Kitchener, Sir, that's who we were talking about." Mr Jake Sourby gave Joe a look of utter contempt. "What do you know about such a fine man as Kitchener?" "Well Sir, my Fathers in the army, he told me all about the war in the letters he sent, and he said that Lord Kitchener spoke to him." Joe thought that talking about his Father would put Mr Sourby off the scent of the bird. Jake Sourby sneered at Joe. "Your Father was probably killed, cannon fodder, like the rest of the idiots. He'll be lying somewhere with his head blown off," and sneering said. "Field Marshall Kitchener spoke to your Father, my arse! Why would anyone as grand as Lord Kitchener want to talk to a common private? Especially you're Father. He's dead as mutton Ford, a bag of bones rotting away, somewhere in France."

Jack Simms, noting the look of hatred on his pal's face towards his tormentor, said.. "Come on Joe lets go." Sourby not finished yet, .waved his arm threateningly towards Joe. . "Go on clear off the pair of you, before you feel my boot up your backsides. I expect you both in class in two minutes."

Both boys, thinking that they would never be free of Mr Sourby and horrible Horace, pretended complete subservience to the Headmaster as they hurried to the classroom. It was best that they got away from the dormitory as quickly as possible, if Sourby caught sight of Kitchener, there was no knowing what the evil so and so would do.

It was the practice of Headmaster of Grimthorpe Hall that all boys should learn gardening, for as he pointed out to the authorities, "Teaching the dear boys all about caring for the plants and flowers would stand them in good stead for when they grew to be men, and leave the security of the Home. They will have a trade under their belts."

Of course the wellbeing of the boys wasn't Sourby's concern, but if he had them out in the garden in all weathers, the weak would no doubt fall ill with pneumonia and die, and he got all the bounty of their hard work for nothing. Why pay a professional to do what the brats did for nothing, besides, he was partial to fresh fruit and vegetables.

Joe and three of the other boys had just finished weeding the flower patch, when there was whoosh of wings. It was Kitchener. He had managed to find his way out of the dormitory. Joe in flap picked up the bird, "You shouldn't be here boy. Go back, go back." There was a loud shout, "Put that vermin down at once Ford and get inside. I will deal with you later!" Joe seeing the danger and noting the anger on Mr Sourby's face, threw Kitchener in the air, "Go on boy, go back home! Please!" In a flash the bird was heading for the nearest tree. Joe, feeling anxious, did as the Headmaster told him, at the same time praying that Kitchener did go home to Magpies Roost.

After the beating, Joe left Mr Sourby's office with a throbbing bottom and more hatred than ever for this man. As he walked away, Joe let the tears fall, he had managed to bite them back in the presence of his enemy, he wouldn't give that pig the satisfaction. Mr Gordon on his way to class, came upon the weeping boy, and realising what had happened, came to Joe's side. "Are you alright Ford?" He asked. Joe, hardly able to speak lowered his head, he felt ashamed and humiliated. It was bad enough having your bum tanned but the indignity of removing your trousers was even more embarrassing, especially when Sourby looked at your, thing, and laughed. That was the worst.

"Come with me Lad, I think Matron ought to take a look at you." Joe shook his head,
"Please Mr Gordon, I'll be alright, don't make me go to Miss Crabtree." But Andrew Gordon was adamant, "I think you should see her Ford, Matron will be able to help you. Come on, it's alright, wait there while I go and have a word with her."

Matron Daphne Crabtree listened while Andrew Gordon informed her of yet another boy who had taken a beating from the sadistic Headmaster. On hearing the too familiar story, she shook her head, "This can't be allowed to continue Andrew, we must put a stop to the cruelty. Show the boy in." When Joe reluctantly bared his bruised bottom to the Matron, the woman was appalled at the extent of the injury. On applying a dressing of arnica, to bring out the bruise, and telling the boy he must rest in bed, Daphne Crabtree decided it was time to confront Mr Jake Sourby about his behaviour towards the boys in his care.

Joe tried to rest in his bed. He found it easier to lie on his stomach, rather than his back. As time went by, Joe was experiencing pain in his back as well as his bottom and his legs ached too. The birch hadn't only, struck his posterior, but where the twigs had landed, wheels of red inflamed flesh were evident on other more delicate parts of his body.

True to her word, Daphne Crabtree confronted the Headmaster, but as usual, the tyrant tried to soft soap the Matron, with the story that the boy had asked for it,
"Ford's insolence won't be tolerated Miss Crabtree. I've warned the lad affore, after all, it could so easily have been you at the receiving end of his tirade of abuse." Adding with a sickly smile. "We cannot allow your delicate ears to be sullied with such filth as came from the boy's mouth."

Matron noting Mr Sourby's attempts to clear himself, and at the same time noticing his piggy eyes mentally undressing her, said what she had gone to say, letting the man know that she didn't believe him and left his office. Once outside the door she shuddered and hurried away. The Headmaster, feeling threatened, struck his desk hard, with a clenched fist.

The boy spent five days and painful nights, on his bed. In the first days Joe was to experience delirium, in his sick state, he was with his Father and Mother in Magpies Roost. But it wasn't the same, Mr Sourby was there, he was beating Kitchener with the birch, blood flying everywhere, his Father was screaming, "One for sorrow Joe." in a maniacal monotone voice. During that time, Jack Simms did his best to keep Joe's spirits up. But the young friend was furious with Sourby, and vowed to make him pay for what he had done to Joe.

Food and drink were brought to Joe. Prepared lovingly for the boy by the cook Nellie Plumly, She too was sick of Sourby's treatment of the boys, besides she had a soft spot for Joe Ford, probably because he seemed always in the line of fire for horrible Mr Sourby. Matron came along with the occasional Beecham's Powder, attention being paid to his injuries, boracic acid in tepid water, used as an antiseptic being applied to the area. Matron Crabtree proved once more, to be a kind person, despite the starchy appearance of uniform and demeanour.

The best thing to happen, however, was that Kitchener paid regular visits, alighting on the balcony outside Joe's dormitory window while the boy was confined to his bed. Although happy to see his friend, it scared Joe, for if the bird was discovered in or around Grimthorpe Hall, there would be hell to pay. Was the awful nightmare he had been experiencing, a warning that something terrible was about to take place? Was it an omen, something to do with his Father or Mother? Perhaps his Granddad wasn't getting better?

Yes, you could say that the nightmare was a warning, but not in the way Joe had envisaged. The lad was right to be concerned about Kitchener. The pigeon had become such a regular visitor to Grimthorpe Hall. He had got used to the place the short time he had been resident the dormitory, that there weren't many people who hadn't seen the bird, or who knew something of the story. Most of the boys and staff thought the story quaint, and watched regularly, for Kitchener's arrival.

Another who watched and waited was Horace Sourby. He'd noticed the pigeon sitting on a certain dormitory windowsill for some time. The bird usually arrived about the same time every day, Horace had wondered, but now he knew the soppy tale, he could use it to take his revenge on Ford. No one made a fool of his Father and got away with it. No one!

At the same time Horace Sourby was plotting his revenge, Joe Ford and Jack Simms had been planning their escape from Grimthorpe Hall. The boys had become such good pals over the past couple of months, sticking up for each other, and covering up for the other, that they decided, when Joe ran away, as he had always intended to do, then Jack would go with him.

Jack Simms fully endorsed what Joe had told him about his Father being alive. Besides, Jack hated Grimthorpe Hall with a passion. He was willing to risk everything to get away from this prison. Not that he had much to loose anyway. But now he had a good pal in Joe Ford, he meant to stick with him. This was to be an adventure, but there was just one more thing he must do, before they left.... and that was to catch the person he suspected of trying to harm Kitchener!

Meanwhile, unaware that he was under suspicion, Horace examined his catapult closely. Holding the strong forked twig with his left hand and pulling back on the sling with his right. "A few stones at a time should do the trick." He mumbled, through clenched teeth.

The evil blighter had worked out, that the best place to kill or injure the pigeon, would be on the roof of Grimthorpe Hall. He'd lived there long enough to know his way around the place, besides, nobody would see him up there. He could use the back stairs onto the roof, no one else knew of their existence, except his Father.

Well, Horace had got that wrong! A certain Jack Simms was very aware of the secret. Staircase. He'd used it to his advantage, on more than one occasion. He would be using it again shortly. But he didn't know it would be sooner than he thought...

The boys had been planning for their escape ever since Joe's last ordeal. It seemed now was as good a time as any to make a move. It was high summer. The weather was warmer, so the boys had decided to leave their jackets behind, meaning less to carry.

Joe had worked out that Magpies Roost would be about three miles away, as the crow flies, the lad was trying to remember how long it had taken to get to Grimthorpe Hall from Wickets Farm by horse and carriage. If he could work it out, then he would be able to estimate, approximately, the time it would take them to walk home to Magpies Roost. It would be difficult travelling across open country, as opposed to the roads, but the boys thought it safer. They had managed between them to get together a few meagre supplies, there was just enough to fit in Joe's canvas bag, this was going to be enough to carry.

The boys decided that a very early start, on their chosen day of escape, was the best plan. If they set off about 4 am everyone would still be sleeping. But for the time being they would, until that special day, keep their heads down, so as not to raise suspicion.

The breakfast bell had gone, all the boys were up and washed and standing by their beds, waiting for inspection. A dirty neck meant no vitals, not that any of the boys enjoyed the thick porridge that was dished up every day, but it was something to fill your belly.

As Joe and Jack were waiting, Jack motioned to his friend, "Kitchener's just arrived." At the same time something hard hit the window behind Joe's bed, the pigeon, startled, gave a squawk of fright and flew, feathers ruffled, off the windowsill.
"Who did that?" The friends looked at each other. Tommy Biddle, who slept across the other side of the room said. "I saw a stone come flying over from that direction" he said, pointing towards the roof. Everyone raised their eyes to where the boy was pointing. "Did you see anyone Tommy?" said Jack . The lad shook his head and answered. "No Jack, but I thought I saw summat up yonder." Tommy pointed towards the roof of Grimthorpe Hall.

Unfortunately for Kitchener, a similar attack was to happen to the bird on three separate occasions, before the culprit responsible for the cruel act was discovered, and punished for his nasty crime.

After the second attack on Kitchener, this time, the stone coming close enough to the bird to clip his wing, the boys thought they had better make their escape, sooner, rather than later. But first, Jack had an idea. If something, or someone, had been seen near the roof of Grimthorpe Hall, at the same time as Kitchener was being targeted, and Tommy had seen something moving in that vicinity. Then, as he knew the way up to the roof, Jack Simms would wait his time, and investigate what was going on. Jack thought he had a pretty good idea who the culprit was, and he was right.

It wasn't long, however, before Jack Simms would be confronting a certain blaguard on the roof of Grimthorpe Hall. The flabby Horace Sourby, intent on harming Kitchener, and out for revenge towards Joe Ford, made a big mistake. The evil blighter knowing what the pigeon meant to Joe had managed somehow to net the poor bird, tempting Kitchener with a tasty morsel of food from the top table. He had thrust him in a sack. Some of the boys who had seen this happen and alerted Joe. "He's taken Kitchener on the roof! Horace Sourby stuffed him in a bag!" Joe, white with fear for his bird, looked at Jack .who said. "Stay here Joe I'll get the rotten sod!" And with that Jack Simms took off like the wind. He raced towards the secret staircase, he knew that it lead to the roof of Grimthorpe. This place had been a hideaway for him when he first came to live here, a place where he could hide away from Mr Sourby, and his beatings.

Jack knew every brick, he even knew of the cellar underneath these stairs, he'd been chucked in there enough times. He climbed the steps quietly, he was careful not to slip on the broken one. There were twenty-six steps, Jack knew, he'd counted them. When he was almost at the top, he could see Horace Sourby. The boy, totally unaware that he had been followed, was sitting on his hunkers eating what looked like a meat pie. Jack felt the hatred for this so and so, rise up in his throat. He would get him and put a stop to his antics, once and for all. At that moment Horace spotted his enemy. The overweight bully struggled to his feet, and grabbed the sack containing Kitchener.

"Come near me Simms, and the pigeon goes over the balcony!" He threatened. Joe, who had followed his pal up the staircase, intent on helping Jack, slipped on the broken step. The yell of pain resonating from Joe's lips was so loud that it took Horace by surprise .The bully dropped the sack on the floor beside him and tried to run. But because of his bulk, Horace didn't get very far, nimble Jack Simms, grabbed the boy by the legs and brought him down. Horace Sourby's squeals could be heard all over Grimthorpe Hall. "Don't hurt me, please don't hit me!" He cried. Jack, seething with anger at Sourby, pulled his arm back, and with a clenched fist gave the bully one smash in the breadbasket. Horace, out for the count; lay where he fell.

Jack picked up the sack expecting to find a dead bird inside, but thank God, apart from a few loose feathers, Kitchener seemed intact. Jack stroked the bird and with a command, "Go home boy. Go home." Kitchener was away to Magpies Roost.

Jack was on his way back down the stairs to see to Joe, when all hell was let loose. The Headmaster, along with other members of staff, was running towards the disturbance. Boys, whooping and hollering at all the excitement, were coming up behind. Jake Sourby, red faced and out of puff, went to his Son's side. "What the hell has been going on here? How did you find this place?" He bellowed. Horace, who was coming round from the knock out, tried to get to his feet, cried, "Ford and Simms made me come up to the roof, Father, the ruffians said they were going to chuck me off!" The Headmaster listened to his simpering offspring, and at this moment, had a strong desire to do just that.

Jake Sourby, feeling embarrassed about his Son's weakness, knowing the boy was probably lying, but blood being thicker than water, and not wishing to loose face, turned to Perks who had beaten him in the run to the roof. "Get my boy to Matron as soon as you can, Ford can wait to be seen." Mr Andrew Gordon who was also on the scene, and disagreeing with the Headmaster that his son, was given first attention, made sure that Joe Ford was seen by Matron as soon as possible.

Joe had suffered a sprained ankle. Matron Crabtree had applied a wet dressing to the injury with a caution. "Rest if you can Lad." But having given this advice, the woman knew it would be impossible, for since this latest melee on the roof between Horace and the two boys in question, Daphne Crabtree didn't hold out much hope, that justice would be done.

In due course he was to get another beating along with Jack, and a warning, that from now on the stairs to the roof were strictly out of bounds.

CHAPTER 5

SEARCHING FOR YOU

Meanwhile, back in the field hospital on the outskirts of Lille, Private 25797 Reuben Ford was beginning to show progress in his recovery. The soldier's physical state   seemed to be responding to treatment, the burns and broken bones heeling well, the mental trauma suffered however, seemed to be taking longer. Reuben, still troubled   by the same persistent nightmare, couldn't understand why this dream haunted his sleep. He felt a prisoner to it, almost every night was the same, he was back at Magpies Roost, standing in the kitchen with Joe, it was a lovely early summer day, as they looked out of the window, a Magpie flew down on to the shed roof. He would call out, "One for sorrow, Joe."   Then another Magpie put in an appearance and Joe would shout out, "Two for joy, Father. Two for joy!"

This had been a game Father and Son played every year, it was an annual event. As the Magpies flew in every spring, to lay their eggs in the tall trees that surrounded Magpies Roost, the cottage so named, because of the Magpie activity in its vicinity. Folklore had it, that a lone Magpie was bad luck, being as they were monogamous by nature, pairing for life. It was deemed good luck to see a pair, thus the game played between Father and Son. Reciting the ditty, 'One for sorrow, two for joy', had become a password between Reuben and Joe. Somehow, seeing two magpies meant everything was alright. They understood its significance, even if no one else did. This included Ruth, who thought her husband and son a pair of dreamers.

But the rhyme was troubling Reuben, What did it mean? Why was he subjected to the ditty almost every night? It must be an omen? Something was wrong, very wrong. Why hadn't he had any news from home? Was home the same? He hadn't received any news from Ruth for weeks. Trouble was, France being so far from home and the war causing havoc, everything that had been normal, wasn't any more.

He must get home or he would go out of his mind. The trouble was, Reuben wasn't out of the woods yet his injuries had been such that he was only now making sense of all he'd gone through. His broken arm and rib were mending, but the injured left leg was taking longer than anticipated to recover. Reuben was getting used to the wheelchair, which was cumbersome and awkward, but at least it gave him a modicum of freedom from the hard hospital bed. Reuben realised he must get well before he could do anything, but because he was in a strange country, hampered by these injuries inflicted on him, by those German invaders, he was like a rat in a trap.

Meantime, back in England at the St Cuthbert's Sanatorium, Mrs Ruth Ford was showing signs of recovery. The mental breakdown had been devastating, the news that Reuben was reported missing, and this information so close to the death of her mother, had been too much to bare.. Ruth found herself in a pit of despair, unable to crawl out, she'd tried, oh yes Ruth had done her best to claw herself out, but the sides of the pit were too shiny, and white, she couldn't get a grip. In fact everything was white, people were walking about in white clothes, they smiled, as the sharp pain stabbed her arm, and bottom. They all spoke the same, slowly in monotone and she didn't like them.

But recently there had been an improvement in the lady. Ruth was able to sit up in bed taking notice of things around her. She noticed the nurses, busy and efficient, everything was neat and starched. Two rows of beds lined and regimented, stood at each side of the ward, most being occupied by traumatised patients. The walls of the ward were covered in white tiles from floor to ceiling. This fact troubled Ruth for some reason she didn't like the white shiny tiles. They frightened her. The reason for this was that during her first weeks, Ruth had managed to get out of bed and was discovered trying to climb the wall by the side of her bed. Heavier sedation was given to prevent this happening. There were other things, about this place, that were troubling Ruth, she didn't like the screaming. She had heard a lot of screaming and moaning, some coming from inside her own head! Why would that be? Ruth remembered the gnarled hand at the side of her bed, the spidery fingers, poking and prodding. It was a living in a nightmare, and she didn't like the smell of vomit and faeces, or the horrible looking woman in the bed opposite her. Staring, staring....

Ruth was beginning to remember something about Reuben and Joe, but where were they? She wanted Reuben, he mustn't be dead. He couldn't be dead!

Ward 7 of   St Cuthbert's Hospital was busy as always. Doctors and nurses were having to deal with traumatised patients, who, one way and another, were suffering the effects of the war. Wives, in the same boat as Ruth Ford, husbands missing, in most cases presumed dead, or mothers weeping for their lost sons. In almost all cases barbiturates were prescribed. Ruth Ford had been given a moderate dose, this no doubt being the cause of her confusion and loss of co-ordination. But it had to be said, Mrs Ford was fortunate in that, her illness was to be temporary. She would recover. Not so, for many of the patients in this hospital. Most of these were lunatics, and imbeciles, who would more than likely, die here.

But now Ruth's illness showed signs of improvement, a lower dose of drugs had been prescribed. Her troubled mind was beginning to clear. How long had she been in this place? Weeks Months? She must find out. Where was her boy? She needed some news. Why wouldn't anybody tell her? Had Reuben been found? She must, know. Well, Ruth, who had always been a matter of fact lady, not given to miracles happening, was in for the shock of her life. A shock, that was to change her way of thinking, forever.

Unbeknown to Ruth Ford, it had been decided by the medical team taking care of her Husband that Reuben would fair better back in England, and he was, at this very moment, making his way to Calais by ambulance. He would be crossing the channel by boat, arriving at Dover he would then be taken to the Military Hospital in Southampton.

Reuben stayed at the Southampton Hospital for two weeks where he was recovering so well, that it was decided, that because of the influx of recent, badly injured war casualties, and the need for beds, Private Ford, could be sent to St Cuthbert's Hospital on the outskirts of Hull to convalesce.

St Cuthbert's was a large building, constructed back in Victorian times, rather archaic and foreboding. It stood in three acres of ground, far too large and ostentatious, built to impress, by Lord somebody or other. The extensive lawns had been taken over recently to house large wooden huts, to be used in the treatment of military personnel, recovering from the trauma of battle and in need of peace and quiet, amidst England's green and pleasant land.

Fate was strange and it was about to weave its magic once more....

The convalescent block was situated at the far end of St Cuthbert's grounds, at the back of the main hospital. It consisted of a scattering of what were intended to be temporary dwellings. These included five hospital blocks, two operating theatres, a canteen, and a bar, much to the delight of most of the lads. This was soon to be named Shangri-la, by some of the more enterprising inmates of the wooden hospital.

Private 25797 Reuben Ford arrived at St Cuthbert's, along with another soldier from the same battalion by the name of Alex Weller. The soldier in question hadn't faired so well, he had lost both legs, while fighting on the front in the battle at Ypres. But the man's dexterity with his wheelchair was something to behold. Reuben liked the man. Alex Weller called a spade a spade, a straight talking Yorkshire man with a good sense of humour, a clever wit, spouted poetry with a passion, and sang a good song, unfortunately mostly out of tune.

Ruth had seen the ambulance coming up the drive and disappearing around the back of the hospital, she supposed it would be going to the military convalescent buildings. Her bed, being by the window, afforded her a good view of the front of St Cuthbert's. She shook her head. That would be another poor soldier injured in the line of duty, Ruth sighed, but at least he was home, not like Reuben, missing in action - feared dead. Oh, they hadn't said that at the time, but Ruth was recovering now, and she was remembering more and more. She had been happy once with a good Mam and Dad, a good husband, and Joe, her boy. Dear God! Where was he? Where was Joe?

Little did Ruth know that her son was an inmate of Grimthorpe Hall, and had been since Eli had suffered his accident. Trouble was. She knew nothing of it, the nervous breakdown along with the medication to treat the condition, had robbed her of thought and memory. All she knew of that time was the pit, and not being able to climb out. White shiny walls, voices talking slowly, and sharp pain in her arms and bottom. The voices had frightened Ruth, they had laughed sometimes, why were they laughing? Ruth wasn't. She couldn't be part of anything outside the pit and anyway she was too tired. Recently, however, she had been feeling better. She was beginning to recall certain facts. But why wouldn't anybody tell her anything? She had asked about Joe. Why couldn't they see she wanted to know about her son? But her questions each time were met with stony silence. For it was thought advisable by hospital staff, not to inform Mrs Ford about Grimthorpe Hall, fearing such news would undo her slow recovery. She would soon, however, learn the facts about her son.

The place was notorious for malpractice, most of the boys who resided in that God forsaken place were orphans, who had slipped through the net, with nobody to speak for them, and as usual, in cases of this kind, any complaint was swept under the carpet. Who cared about a few unwanted orphans in all the mayhem of a world war? People were dying all around, what difference did a few more make?

Three people who worked at Grimthorpe Hall cared. They had been concerned for some time, Matron Daphne Crabtree, Mr Andrew Gordon, the Housemaster and Mr Perks, the porter come handy man. These three people had been well aware for some time about the malpractice going on at Grimthorpe. But soon, things were about to come to a sticky end for a certain Headmaster and his nasty son.

Eli Jennings was getting used to walking with crutches, the blasted things were cumbersome, the tops digging into his armpits like nobodies business, chafing and rubbing, but they did give a measure of support, enabling him to walk a little. He was soon to be discharged from the hospital, and there were two thing's he intended to do, go and visit his daughter at St Cuthbert's and fetch Joe out of Grimthorpe Hall.

To say Eli had been worried was an understatement. He had felt like a prisoner to his feeble body, young chits of nurses washing and powdering his privates! It wasn't fitting, even

Kate had never had to suffer the embarrassment of washing him down there, except when he had suffered that boil, between the cheeks of his bum, and then, it had been a hot bread poultice slapped on the offending yellow headed blighter, and a quick wash round with a flannel. No it wasn't right for young bits of girls, but enough about that, he would soon be on his way to visit Ruth. Eli knew it wasn't going to be easy, hiding the truth about Joe being in that awful place. But what was he to do? He blamed Jethro and Grace Wickets for this. They should have persevered with Joe, especially in the circumstances, he should never have been sent to that hellhole. But the lad wouldn't be there much longer, Eli would see to that, just as soon as he was fit enough to cope.

Eli had been home for almost a week, and was managing to hobble around with his crutches. They were cumbersome but at least Magpies Roost, being larger than the cottage he and Kate had shared, meant he was able to move around that little bit better. Oh how he missed his Kate, if she had still been here, things wouldn't be in this state. The boy would be with them, not in that bloody awful place. Eli could hardly wait to get Joe home, but he must see Ruth first. The thing was. Should he tell her or not? If he did, how would she take the news that her boy had been in that vile hole for all these weeks? Eli pondered the question and decided, that he would tell Ruth when he visited her at the hospital, but only if, she was well enough to hear the truth.

The old man couldn't make the stairs yet, but the blacksmith had been kind enough to bring the mattress down from his bedroom, it made the horsehair sofa a bit more comfortable, especially now his hip was giving him such pain. Eli found the lavvy a bit daunting, the old path leading to it in the back garden, left a lot to be desired, but he managed, with a few accidents here and there! Eli was also grateful for the food Bill Jobson brought him. The blacksmith was a dab hand at making a good stew, be it rabbit, pigeon or mutton, the homemade cider was also accepted with thanks. Eli was partial to a drop apple cider.

Bill Jobson was happy to oblige, when Eli asked if he could take him to St Cuthbert's, it had been some time since Ruth Ford was taken bad. He missed her, mind you! he wasn't surprised the woman had lost her mind, what with Reuben missing in France and her mam dying. He wasn't sure just how much more the lady could take or what she knew. Unfortunately, the blacksmith still carried a torch for the lass, and when the news had come of her breakdown and subsequent internment into the hellhole that was St Cuthbert's, Bill Jobson was beside himself with grief. Why hadn't he persevered with the lad? He could at least have spared Ruth the pain of her boy being in that God forsaken Grimthorpe Hall, curse his bloody selfishness!

The horse and trap was waiting outside. Bill was helping Eli up into the seat, when they saw the pigeon fly round the back of Magpies Roost. The blacksmith motioned to Eli, "He's here again, back and forth, back and forth. Do you reckon that's the one the Lad calls Kitchener? Funny he's on his own, must have lost his mate, perhaps he's looking for the Lad? They were always close, strange that."

Eli knew the pigeon was Kitchener, he'd been watching him. He'd noticed the bird on the roof of Magpies Roost, directly above the coop, almost as soon as he came out of hospital. It was something to do with the lad it had to be. For since he had been home, Eli reckoned, the pigeon seemed to be on a mission. He was arriving and leaving at the same time almost every day, and by the looks of the droppings on the floor by the pigeon coop, 'Kitchener,' Eli was convinced that's who the pigeon was, had been coming back and forth all the time he had been in hospital with a broken hip.

St Cuthbert's looked imposing, a massive building, holding so much pain and misery within its walls. Its huge facade was a forbidding presence, looming large in the picturesque North Yorkshire landscape, and for those people fortunate enough never to step over the threshold of St Cuthbert's, were to be spared a peep into hell.

The blacksmith gently pulled on the reigns and the horses stopped in the drive. The journey had been pleasant as it was full summer. They had passed fields of ripening golden corn, pretty gardens sporting colourful flowers. Children playing in the streets, seemingly oblivious of the war, and the heartache it caused. Eli knew all about heartache, there were many kinds, and he'd suffered a few. He mused to himself, how could the sun shine so beautifully, on a world at war? By rights it should be pouring down with rain, sunshine made a mockery, of the hell many people were feeling.

Time, two thirty in the afternoon, Eli would soon be in that terrible place, and he mouthed again, "God help my daughter." Bill Jobson gave Eli a hand down from the cart. Both men walked towards the imposing building and in through the large wooden doors. The first thing to hit was the strong smell of urine, the thick stench seemed to go up the nose, and stick in the back of your throat. Both men walked along the dark corridor, which lead to the part of the hospital where Mrs Ruth Ford had been for the past few months. They stepped into the ward, to be greeted by a starchy face nurse, who unsmiling, showed them to the bed occupied by Ruth. "Visiting is half an hour only." Said, the nurse, Eli nodded his thanks, and turning to Bill Jobson, said "Sounds like she's got a plum in her mouth, stuck up bitch." The blacksmith, knowing all about Eli and his caustic remarks, took hold of the old man's arm, and lead him in the direction of his daughter's bed, leaving the nurse to mull over the rude comments.

Fortunately for Ruth, if fortunate is the word to use, she never saw the wards where lunatics and imbeciles were housed. She was on occasion, able to hear horrible noises coming from somewhere nearby, especially during the night. Or were the frightening sounds actually inside her own head, and part of her own nightmares? At times she hadn't felt sure. It had all been fearful muddle to Ruth, but now she was on the mend, she was beginning to understand what had happened to her, and why.

Ruth caught sight of her father and the blacksmith as they entered the ward, Eli hobbled to his daughter's bedside. The girl threw her arms around her Eli's neck. "Oh Dad! What's happened? Where have you been? Have you brought Joe? Where's Joe? I've been ill Dad, I want Reuben!" Ruth, overcome, broke into tears, "Tell me what happened Dad, please? Why didn't you bring my boy? I want my son!" She cried. Eli, desperately wandering what to do, looked round at Bill Jobson. The blacksmith, knowing what should be done, spoke to Eli, "Tell her man, she's a right to know where her Lad is. Just tell the girl." Eli felt his mouth go dry, where was he supposed to start? How would Ruth take the news that Joe was at Grimthorpe Hall? His daughter had always known of its presence, and reputation, but never in a million years, would she have thought that her own son would be an inmate of that terrible place.

The old man began, telling of how Grace and Jethro Wickets had offered to take Joe in. But because they had been unable to prevent the lad from going back to Magpies Roost at every opportunity he could find, with the excuse he must be at the Cottage for when his dad came back, they reluctantly had to let him go into the home. Jethro was worn out chasing back and forth in search of the boy. Ruth listened to her Dad as he spoke of this horror that had befallen her son. She looked up at the blacksmith.

"Couldn't you have taken Joe in for a time? The Lad's no trouble." Ruth turning to her father, said. ."How long has he been in that God forsaken place?" Eli feeling less than worthless answered his daughter. "About five months now." It was the turn of Bill Jobson, to feel shame faced, especially now he had experienced the gut wrenching horror of actually being inside of this terrible place. Why hadn't he persevered with the boy? He should have tried a bit harder, he could have prevented some of the woman's anguish. Why, oh why? Dear God above. Why?

The inside of this building epitomised everything that was bad. The stench, the ominous feel of foreboding was everywhere, and he could have done more. He should have taken care of the boy. Knowing Joe was safe with him may have hastened the recovery for Ruth. Apparently, according to Eli, Ruth had asked about her boy even when she had been demented, only to be told nothing. The blacksmith felt the guilt envelope him.

Ruth, shocked at what she had just been told, screamed at her Father, "Five months! Five months! Oh my boy! Good God above. Go and fetch him out of that awful place. Please Father, go and get him!" With that Ruth passed out cold.

Eli and Bill, in a panic called hospital staff. They were asked to leave and as the curtains were pulled round Ruth's bed, medical personnel, administered drugs to the collapsed patient, and gently laid her down.

Eli and Bill left the hospital. The old man felt sick! What had he done? He must get well, as soon as he could, get rid of these accursed crutches and go and bring the boy home. He would write to the Headmaster, and tell him of his plans to collect Joe and bring him home. But little did Eli know just how terrible conditions had been for his Grandson whist residing in this so-called, 'church run children's home.' But he was about to find out, and when he did, there would be hell to pay.

There were also plans afoot at Grimthorpe Hall. Jack Simms had taken a beating, accused of stealing food. He had been seen pocketing a chunk of dry bread, by no other than, Horace Sourby, who was only too happy to report the incident to his Father. Of course the food had been for the pigeon, but no matter, Simms was a thief and would be punished accordingly. That was Mr Jake Sourby's view on the situation. They got what they deserved. He hated the lot of um.

This latest birching had been the last straw. Matron Crabtree had seen enough bruised bottoms, hurt pride, and tears, to last her a lifetime. Something had to be done and she was about set the wheels in motion.

Wheels had also been turning in Joe Ford's head. Ever since this latest assault on his friend and himself, so, as soon as Jack was well enough to travel and he felt fit enough, they would both be off. They were recovering well. Matron Crabtree had worked her magic once more, applying soothing balm on the angry red scars caused by the cruel beating, and reapplying the dressing on Joe's leg.

She had asked herself again, how much longer this mindless violence would be allowed to continue? Times were hard, with the atrocities of war and all that entailed going seemingly unheeded, death and injury being part and parcel of life today. But someone must take a stand! She had tried to reason with the Headmaster, but her heartfelt plea had fallen on deaf ears. Mr Gordon was of the same mind as was Mathew Perks the porter. But in the bedlam that was war, hardship being the order of the day, it would seem that evil Mr Jake Sourby had sweet talked himself out of any enquiry alluding to his mismanagement of the boys in his care.

Daphne Crabtree wasn't at all surprised when, after being discharged from her care, her latest young patient's had gone missing.

CHAPTER 6

THE DEN IN THE WOODS

The boys had practised and memorised every last detail of their escape. It would work,they had been planning it for a long time. They must succeed! Joe didn't fancy a repeat performance of the beating he and Jack had suffered last time. This was to them a 'do or die' situation, neither boy prepared to suffer any more of Sourby's cruelty, they had each other. Their chances of freedom would be assured. The long awaited day of escape was looming. They had tried to sleep, but both boys found it near impossible. Jack leaning across to Joe's bed, whispered, "Its nearly light Joe, I'm getting up." Joe, wide-awake, nodded, they both knew what had to be done. It was late summer, that meant it would be daylight around four am, the boys had worked out this was as good a time as any, to make their bid for freedom, everyone would hopefully be asleep. They had planned their escape from this place with meticulous accuracy.

The boys were relieved that Kitchener had been sent ahead, the bird would be safely home by now. As they had decided to travel light, the rations were meagre, just enough to fill Joe's canvas bag. This consisted of a few bits of veg from the garden, some chunks of bread, stale now, and a large bruised apple. The boots would be carried over their shoulder until they had left the vicinity of Grimthorpe Hall.

All was quiet, most boys sleeping, except the few who knew of the escape plan. These boys were wide eyed, but remained in their beds, none wanted to be involved, for fear of reprisals, but they were envious of the tenacity their friends exhibited. Some were near to tears, not wanting to loose the escapee's, but wishing them well anyway.

As the pair reached the front door, there was a noise. It was Mr Perks. The porter, come odd job man, was just coming out of the sick room carrying a bundle of bedding, and judging by the look on the man's face, there must have been a death. It struck Joe that it was probably the young lad that had come in the other day, from the workhouse. No one had set eyes on him since because he had been hurried into the sick room. Poor thing, he was just another waif whom nobody wanted.

Mr Perks, looking sad faced, owing no doubt to the task he had just undergone, whispered to the boys. "Where do you think you are going? If Sourby catches you you'll be for the high jump." Joe looked Mr Perks full in the face. "Pretend you haven't seen us, we're running away. I know a place where we can hide. Please don't tell on us Mr Perks, please." The hapless porter, knowing in part what these boys had suffered since living in this hell-hole, nodded his understanding, and with a cautionary word of warning, bib the boys farewell, half wishing he had the bottle to do likewise. Mr Perks, not really being of Christian persuasion, but admired the boys' spirit, sent up a prayer to God, if he was there, asking him to keep an eye on Ford and Simms.

Quietly and with stealth, the lads were out of the door. Joe, remembering which way to go, led the way down the drive. Nobody was about and all was quiet. There was a mist on the ground, which meant warm weather later. The morning chorus was all around them, birds knowing nothing of the horror within the walls of Grimthorpe, sang their little hearts out, happy to greet a new day. Among the sweet voices of blackbird, robin and thrush, Joe detected a familiar call, raucous and chittering, the sound coming from a tall oak tree, directly in front of them. Joe raised his head, and looking at the Magpie, he whispered, "One for sorrow, Joe," and from deep within his inner being he prayed the words, and gave the answer, "two for joy, Father."

Jack, looking on, said, "Are you alright, Joe?" The boy put his wandering thoughts away, and nodded to Jack. They had reached the main gate of Grimthorpe unchallenged, except for Mr Perks, thank Gods it was him and not Mr Sourby, otherwise the outcome would have been fearsome if that rogue had got wind of the escape.

The boys crossed the road, and climbed over the fence, if they could make it to the fields along side the back of the home, they would have a chance. None of Grimthorpe Hall staff lived overlooking the back of the property. That was where the inmates were housed, out of sight and mind.

The boys kept low. Luckily for them the corn hadn't been cut yet, so the field of golden sunshine gave cover in a most natural way. Half way across the next field about an hour into their escape, the boys decided to take a breather, luckily, the sun was still pretty low in the azure blue sky. Poppies that grew in profusion amongst the stalks of corn, were beginning to show their blood red petals.

Joe opened his canvas bag, as by now, both of them were hungry. Jack took a huge bite from the stale bread and he ate ravenously. They shared the bruised apple, both appreciating the moisture from the juice. Jack looked at his pal enquiringly. said "How much further before we reach the wood?" Joe, not exactly sure, just how much further they would have to travel, shook his head. "I can't be certain, I know the wood, but I've never approached it from this angle. It's a massive place, about twenty acres, but don't worry Jack, I'll know where to find the Den when I get my bearings."

Around the time the boys reached the edge of Bluebell Wood, the alarm bells were ringing back at Grimthorpe Hall. Luckily for the escapee's, it had been a good hour since they had absconded, thus, giving the pair a good start. Mr Sourby, when informed of the boys prank, as well as seething with anger, felt pretty scared.

"They must be found at once, they may be in difficulty." These were the words spouting from the Headmaster's mouth, but the truth was, his heart was black with rage. If they got away, and opened their mouths, his lucrative job as Headmaster of Grimthorpe Hall would be finished, he would be a gonna and he knew it. At this point however, he didn't see any need to involve the authorities, or the police.

"No, no," he had said to his Housemaster, when the suggestion had been made.

"Far better we attend to the problem ourselves, we don't want any trouble do we Mr Gordon?" But Mr Andrew Gordon knew full well, that Sourby didn't want the police involved because of his malpractice in managing Grimthorpe Hall, and the mistreatment doled out by him, to the unfortunate boys living within these dark walls.

The Housemaster, along with the Matron and Mr Perks, had fought a loosing battle for years, trying to protect vulnerable boys from abuse. That blighter Sourby always came up smelling of roses each time there was an enquiry. Perhaps now, with the escape of Ford and Simms, there was light at the end of a long tunnel, and the truth, about what really went on in this dreadful place would come out. But did anybody in authority really care what happened to the number of orphans residing here? The world was at war, everything in chaos, what did it matter about what went on at Grimthorpe Hall?

Well, unbeknown to Mr Sourby, the balloon was about to go up. For as Joe Ford and Jack Simms were making their bid for freedom, Eli Jennings and Bill Jobson were making arrangements to visit Grimthorpe Hall. Eli had written a letter to the Headmaster, some time ago, telling the man of his intention to take his Grandson out of the children's home. Eli had received a very flowery letter back, telling him that the boy was well thought of, and would be sadly missed. Eli had felt uncomfortable at the reply, he had heard rumours about the Hall, and nothing had been proved however, as to the mismanagement of the Home. But in Eli's view, there was no smoke without fire, rumours didn't just materialise out of thin air.

It was now almost a full day since the boys had made their escape. So whilst Mr Sourby and his staff were becoming increasingly concerned, one because he was frightened out of his mind at what would happen to him, and the genuinely worried staff, who feared for Fords and Simms safety. Mr Gordon's plea to the Headmaster, that the police should be contacted, had fallen on deaf ears. The man was worried, he had asked some of the boys if they knew anything, but he was met with closed lips. If any boy knew where Ford and Simms had gone, they weren't saying.

Meanwhile, Joe and Jack were about halfway through Bluebell Wood, the late evening sun was glinting between the branches of the canopy. The boys estimated the time to be about seven. They had passed a stream, and tasting the water, found it to be sweet, the boys drank their fill. Jack eager to get to their destination asked "How much further to the Den Joe? Hope it's not too far from the stream?" Joe looked at his friend, "Not much further now, I remember the water, Father and me had a paddle here once." The lad sighed, "Father loved the wood, I wish he was with us now." The boys pressed on knowing they must find the Den before nightfall. They had been fortunate to find an old withered apple tree that still had some fruit on the branches, grub eaten, but the taste was beautiful. As they came to a particularly overgrown patch of undergrowth, Joe stopped, "This is it Jack!   I remember the two giant oak trees growing side by side." Joe began to clamber through the thicket, "Its in there, the Den is behind the oak tree on the right!" Jack followed his pal through the undergrowth, he looked up at the pair of massive oak trees, it was as though they were standing sentinel and proud. They knew a secret, and it was their secret. Joe pressed forward, "Come on Jack, its round the back." The oak in question was at least nine feet in circumference, the boys stepped around its perimeter.

Jack awestruck now by what was before him, remarked to his friend, "Look at the size of that trunk! What a Den. Did you play here much?" Joe nodded, "Yes quite a lot. My Granddad helped to make it. Come on, let's go and have a look."

The opening in the trunk was roughly about four feet wide. It was completely invisible from view, as the opening was at the back. The trees stood in front of the only wall in the wood, the wall in question was very old, crumbling in part, Joe remembered his Granddad saying something about a garden, and an old ruin at the other side of the structure. He remembered talk of a secret passageway through a gate but he couldn't remember where it was, or if it even existed.

The hole in the tree trunk was large enough for one small person to climb inside. Over the years, debris and other rubbish had collected in the opening, worn larger now with the passage of time, and harsh weather. By the smell, Joe reckoned a badger, or fox had made the tree cavity his home at some time. The trunk was hollow, rotted inside, but still alive, this fact being obvious by the abundance of leaves up in the highest branches.

Both boys had managed to get inside, and could quite easily sit comfortably. It was quite dry and surprisingly warm. This secret Den was to prove a God send, for they would be here for quite a time. They drew comfort from the fact, that nobody would ever be able to find them here. Grimthorpe Hall was well and truly behind them, for good. The lads rested, it had been a long day, they were both tired and hungry but they must sleep for a while. They would search for food later.

Eli and Bill arrived at Grimthorpe Hall, to be met by blind panic. The two visitors were hurried into Mr Sourby's office. The Headmaster, sweating profusely, tried to explain how and why the two boys felt they had to leave this place of safety.

"Let me assure you, Mr Jennings, everything is being done to ensure that the dear boys come back home without delay. I must tell you that no stone will be left unturned in our endeavour to bring the boys back to the haven that is Grimthorpe Hall."

Eli Jennings listened to the tubby man spouting all the honey from his slobbery lips.

"You say the boys ran away yesterday?" Sourby gave Eli a nod. Then Eli said "Why the hell haven't you called the Police? The boys could be dead in a gutter by now!" Eli could feel his hackles rising. The headmaster, looking ashen said "We wanted to keep the investigation private, didn't see any need to involve the authorities." Eli, seething with anger, retaliated, "Like hell you did, you bloody liar!" And seeing red now, said "Get in touch with them at once! I'm warning you Sourby, if anything happens to my Grandson, I'll thrash you within an inch of your wretched life! Just don't try your soft soap on me, Sourby, cos it doesn't wash."

A, now gibbering excuse for a man, knowing that his goose was probably well and truly cooked, tried to placate his adversary, "Now, Mr Jennings, I feel sure that the boys will come home of their own accord. It's merely a prank on their part. After all, they have a splendid home here at Grimthorpe. Why would the boy's wish to leave this fine establishment?" Sourby knew he was playing for time. Jennings couldn't prove anything against him, others had tried without success, to bring him down, but up to now, he had managed to cover his tracks pretty well.

With no further ado, the blacksmith, being nimble on his feet and sick of hearing the slobbering liar, rushed towards the

Headmaster, and grabbing the man by the throat. "You heard what Mr Jennings said Sourby! Get the police at once, or God help me, I'll wipe the floor with you!" At that moment the office door opened, and the Housemaster walked in, followed by Matron Crabtree. The blacksmith loosened his grip on Sourby's flabby neck and rubbed his hand down his breeches as though wanting to rid himself of the feel of the tyrant.

Mr Sourby, spluttering with rage and indignation, at being manhandled in such a way, shouted at the uninvited visitors, "Get out of my office Mr Gordon, and you Matron, can do likewise. Go on, get out!" Mr Gordon, completely ignoring the command to leave put a steadying hand on Daphne Crabtree's arm, bade her to sit down, and turning towards Eli Jennings and the Blacksmith, "Its alright gentlemen, the police are on their way. I heard the rumpus and took it upon myself to call them." With that, quick as a flash, Sourby made a bolt for the door, and considering his weight, he managed puffing and panting, to make it to the staircase which lead to the roof. Three steps up and his son Horace, who was coming the other way, knocked him onto his backside.

Young Sourby, on hearing all the commotion, had fled to the balcony, his intention had been to shin down the drainpipe into his room and lock the door. Unfortunately for the lad, he suffered a similar affliction to his father, he was far too obese to attempt the drainpipe, and had tried to make his escape down the staircase, just as his Father, was making his assent.

Mr Perks, fully aware at what was going on, answered the knock on the front door. Two policemen in full uniform stepped inside. Mr Perks, knowing whom they wanted to see, ushered the two men towards the Headmaster's office. Statements were taken. Mr Sourby, who by now felt like a piece of wet rag, tried to sweet talk his way out of the situation he'd caused, but his lies fell on deaf ears, the officers of the law had heard it all before.

The two policemen prepared to leave, promising that the search for the boys would begin at dawn tomorrow. Their parting shot, aimed at the Headmaster, "No doubt, when we find the boys, the truth as to what has been going on in this establishment will finally come out. Then we will see what's to do." The Yorkshire police officers scrutinised Mr Sourby, they had both been at this job long enough, to know they were dealing with a wrong un.

Eli and the blacksmith, said their farewell to Mr Gordon, and the Matron, but not before they had threatened Sourby once more. The man was finished, bar the shouting, and he knew it.

Now steps had been taken to begin looking for Joe Ford and Jack Simms. The search for the runaways began in earnest. From where Grimthorpe Hall was situated, there were three possible routes the boys could have taken, one was across Shooters Moor, but it was thought too exposed and barren for the boys to attempt that way, then there was the road that would take them to Barrowby, and finally Bluebell Wood. But this was discounted because of the rough terrain between Grimthorpe and the Wood besides people had been known to get lost in the ten acres of dense undergrowth that was Bluebell Wood.

So the search of the chosen area began. Barrowby Road ran parallel with the river, which meandered through meadows and fields before making its way to the tiny Hamlet of Sneeford, where it widened, before making its way to the sea. Two days into the search, and the Police drew a blank. They had left no stone unturned on Barrowby Road in order to locate the missing boys. The sinking feeling shared by most of the searchers was that the boys had come to a watery end. This they felt couldn't be ruled out.

The hunt was shifted to Shooters Moor. The Moor was a barren place, eerie, and soulless. It had at one time been a coalmine, but as the pit had been worked out ages ago, the Moor was now a haven for foxes, badgers and rabbits. Quite safe from mans gun. Nobody wished to set foot in such a foreboding place, not even for a tasty rabbit. Police and volunteers formed a line and proceeded to walk every inch of Shooters Moor leaving no stone unturned in their search for the two boys. When it came to the third day, and still there was no sign of Joe or Jack, the searchers began to think the worst. Eli and the blacksmith had joined the volunteers, who were beside themselves with fear. Had the boys fallen down one of the mineshafts? And if they had, how would they get them out?

As each of the holes in the ground, was discovered, volunteers and Police alike, hollered as loud as they could. Each of the boys' names was called out in turn, but no answer came back. If the boys had fallen into one of the mineshafts they were probably dead by now. All seemed gloom and despondency, but they mustn't give up! Eli couldn't accept the fact that the boys had come to harm, he had one last shot up his sleeve, and a prayer in his heart.

"Why don't we try Bluebell Wood? Eli said. "I know it's vast and can be dangerous, but I have an idea." Eli felt that if the lads were anywhere, it would be there. He was recalling a "Den" that he had helped to construct for Ruth and Reuben along with some other children. It had been a long time ago, but he remembered Joe asking to be taken there, when he was a small boy. Admitted it was a long way from here, the den being almost at the edge of the woods on the far side. But Eli felt in his bones that he was right. So, it was decided, by police and all involved in the search, that this was the only option left.

The boys were coping quite well considering that by now the amount of food they had managed to bring with them had gone. Luckily they were surrounded by nature's bounty. Whilst they had been in Bluebell Wood, their exploring had taken them beyond the old wall. The boys had noticed a small door in the wall just beyond the two giant oak trees, one of which housed the Den. They had managed to gain entrance through the gnarled old gate by pushing and pulling until they gained access. There they had found a veritable treasure chest. Joe remembered his Granddad speaking of a thatched cottage and gardens, but he hadn't envisaged anything quite like this. It was as though the boys had stepped back in time. They were in a walled garden, Joe, through hushed whispers, as though fearful of being overheard. "What do you make of this Jack? Do you reckon anyone lives here?" Jack, almost dumbstruck, looked around him. "Don't know, but can you see all those apples? There must be millions!" Joe thinking that was probably an exaggeration, looked anyway. "And what about the blackberries?" said an overenthusiastic Jack, who proceeded to make his way towards the loaded bush, his tummy dictating the hasty action. Joe, more cautious, "Hang on Jack, we don't know if this belongs to anyone." Joe didn't think this was the case, as everything was overgrown with weeds, but all the same, it would be better to take it steady, and look around carefully before they started helping themselves to anything. Jack, ravenous, couldn't resist a tasty looking apple though, stolen or otherwise.

The boys clambered through the under growth which was waist high in some parts. They walked amongst the trees of apple and pear, loaded to bursting with ripe and overripe fruit. Jack in a whisper, said, "I don't reckon anyone lives here Joe, they can't do, look at the broken down shed over there. With all those empty boxes stacked at the side, half of them broken, and covered in cobwebs. These trees haven't been tended for years."

The boys walked on tentatively until they came to a thatched cottage, Joe stopped.

"My Father told me about this place, a long time ago." Just then from the thatched roof there came a familiar sound. Joe looked to where the chittering noise had come from. "It's a Magpie Jack. Look, up on the roof." Jack nodded his recognition, and Joe, being reminded of his Father once again, all of a sudden, felt very sad. Jack sensing the anguish, tried to comfort his pal, "Come on Joe, your Father will come home soon, and you will be there to meet him, you'll see." Joe hoped his pal was right, it had been many long months of waiting, and hoping, but he knew Jack was doing his best to chivvy him along.

Joe, trying to see the bright side, "Are we going in then?" Jack nodded eager to see the inside of the old cottage. The boys walked towards the wooden door, which was situated in the centre wall, there were three windows at the front, one either side of the door and one under the eves. The thatch seemed almost to touch the tiny window above all three, were dressed with leaded light, and appeared to be nestling comfortably into the thick house walls. It looked as though these had originally been whitewashed, but over time had weathered, and now were a dirty beige colour.

Joe knocked, he didn't know why, for it was pretty obvious that nobody lived there. He banged his knuckles on the door again. Nothing! Jack becoming impatient said to his pal "Come on Joe, the place is empty." Joe lifted the latch and pushed, as he did so there was a creaking sound, the old door swung slowly open. They stepped warily inside. They were standing in a small room, devoid of furniture except for a rocking chair and an old rusty iron bed. There was a small fireplace, and on a shelf, a tin box and a cooking pot with the remains of what must have been the last meal there, and judging by the dust and debris in the fire grate, that must have been a very long time ago.

To the side of the fireplace there was door, Jack, inquisitive, "Wonder what's behind that?" On investigation, the boys found a staircase "Let's go up Joe." Joe feeling a little scared, "Do you think we should? This cottage must belong to somebody." Jack full of bravado, "Come on, this is better than the Den, nobody will find us here."
But Joe was worried, he didn't want to stay here, he wanted to get back to Magpies Roost, and wait for his Father.

When they reached the top of the narrow staircase, they found themselves in a tiny room it was completely bare. The window under the eves looked out onto the overgrown garden. "Why don't we stay here for a while?" said Jack, "It's nice and dry. We could try to catch a rabbit, get some water from the stream, and make a stew. There are loads of cabbages and potatoes in the garden. Come on Joe, let's get our strength back, then we can press on to Magpies Roost?"

The boys went downstairs and sat on the iron bed. On looking through the bare springs Joe noticed on the floor, what looked like a metal handle? On investigation, it turned out to be a lever that opened a trap door. This in turn led down into a small room, dank and dark and by the smell! The boys reckoned it must at one time have been the fruit cellar.

It was now three days since Joe Ford and Jack Simms had absconded from Grimthorpe Hall. The search had so far drawn a blank, but two people were on their trail, convinced that they would find the missing pair. Eli, had one more avenue to explore, if the boys weren't there, then he would have to give up. But he felt, in his innermost being, that the boys would be found in that location. They had to be!

Shooters Moor had been gone over with a fine toothcomb, as had Barrowby Road. The police were ready to call it a day, convinced that the runaways had drowned in the river, or fallen down one of the old mineshafts, dotted about the Moor.

And to be honest, in their view, did anyone really care? The world was at war. People were being misplaced, lost, and killed. The heart seamed to have gone out of caring. It was survival that mattered. The weak went to the wall. The strong fought their way through

Well Eli Jennings wasn't about to go to the wall just yet, he had too much on his plate to go down that particular road. He had a Grandson to find, and a daughter to make well. One was no good without the other. Eli doubted that his son-in-law would ever be found, but that was a tragedy of war, 'Missing, presumed dead,' like countless other poor beggars in this hellish conflict between decent man in his endeavour to bring peace to a hurting world, and the forces of evil, who wanted supremacy.

With meaningful persuasion, Eli was able to get the police and volunteers to turn their search to Bluebell Wood. The police chief wasn't convinced that the boys had taken that particular route. The woods were vast and dark, a daunting place, not fit to venture into, unless you knew what you were doing. Well Eli was pretty certain that his Grandson had gone that way. The police should have listened to him in the first place instead of going bull at a gate into places that Eli was convinced Joe would not have ventured into.

The hunting party had reached the edge of Bluebell Wood. Time was, six am. The morning was dry, much to the relief of the all concerned. It was decided that they should split up, and go in three groups, one centre, and the others, either side of the wood. with each party taking a gun with them which would only be fired as a signal when, the boys were found.

 The runaways, who had decided that fish would be nice for breakfast this morning, were busy with twig and twine. The bits of wire from the apple boxes had made a passable hook, also the biggest worm they could find. Jack had had the job of fixing the hapless worm onto the makeshift fishing hook, Joe felt sorry for the poor thing. But they had to eat. After what seemed ages, the lads had managed to catch two tiddlers and a bigger fish they couldn't name.

Back at the cottage, they very soon got the pot on the fire. The fish went in wholesale along with water from the stream and a couple of carrots and a chopped up potato from the garden. Before long the pot was bubbling, and the aroma of fish stew permeated the cottage, and smoke belched out of the chimney.

The searchers had reached a quarter of the way through Bluebell Wood. Each party, finding difficulty with the harsh terrain, for besides the dense trees and little or no footpath, they had insects biting at their faces and any exposed part of their bodies. Some of the volunteers had grown despondent, fearing this search to be a waste of time, and in fact, two of the more delicate souls had turned back, well, it wasn't their boys missing was it? Luckily for them, they hadn't been in Eli's group. He had little or no time for shirkers, and he would be having a few harsh words for Lilly livered blighters later. After all, he didn't find combing through this wood very easy, in fact his leg was hurting like hell, but he couldn't give in, not till his Grandson and friend were safe.

As the searching groups gradually made their way through Bluebell Wood, scratched, sweating, and bleeding from thorn bushes and insect bites, it was obvious that the team taking the right hand avenue were on the correct path. For it seemed to everyone that this was a well-used path, or had been at one time, for although overgrown there was evidence of tracks beneath the weeds and bracken, that had at one time, been a regular walkway. Eli, one of the police officers, and a volunteer had the enviable pleasure of a semi decent path, once they had bashed through the undergrowth with sturdy sticks.

At last, after four hours of walking, stumbling and swearing, Eli, and the team came to a clearing in the wood. Eli looked up into the branches of the mighty oak trees. Exited, and tired, the old man cried out, "This is it! The den! I recognize the Den!"

The policeman stepped towards the trees, "Where? I can't see anything." Eli, feeling really done in now, pointed at the largest of the oak trees, "It's behind there, go round the back, and you'll see." The policeman did as the old man had suggested, followed by Sam Turnbull, the volunteer, there was silence, then "Well I'll be blowed, did you ever?" There was evidence that someone had been there, but the Den was empty. Eli felt sick, he had been sure the boys would be here, but they weren't. Where could they have got to? But just as all appeared to be lost, there was a cry from Sam Turnbull. "Where's that smoke coming from? See, over there?" The group looked to where the pall of smoke was coming from. Eli felt his heart miss a beat. "Joe lad, are you there? Please be in the cottage?"

Eli knew all about the thatched cottage. In its hay day, before Molly Butterworth passed on, the orchards and garden had provided the old girl with a tidy income, enough in fact to enable her to employ Ned Mason as picker and packer. There had been talk round and about, that Mason swindled Molly Butterworth out of hundreds of pounds. Apparently the gardener had been robbing Molly for years, and as a final act the rogue took a cartload of apples and pears to the local Market, and cleared off with the proceeds. Story went that the old girl never got over it. She was found dead in her bed, and having no living relatives, she was buried in a pauper's grave. Due no doubt, to the fact that the gardener had been systematically robbing Molly for years, and when she died she was virtually penniless. The cottage was locked up and left to the elements. Mason was caught, and tried for his crime.

Eli prayed quietly to himself "Please God, let my boy be in the old cottage. Please!" The search party filled with renewed vigour pressed on towards where they could see the smoke. Eli, recalling the door in the now, crumbling wall, signalled to the police officer. "Through there, go through the old door." Sam Turnbull, half remembering the tale of the old thatched cottage, stepped forward. "I remember summat about that place, the old girl who lived there got robbed. The place is supposed to be derelict." He and the police officer, pushed on the old door, and with a creak and a groan it swung open. The police Sergeant, not wanting to be undermined, took charge. "Step back Turnbull, I will go first, it may not be safe." The search party found themselves in the cottage garden. It was very overgrown, but by the look of fresh disturbance among the vegetable patch and fruit orchard, it would seem they were on the right track.

The boys had almost finished their fish meal. They reckoned it was alright, albeit rather tasteless and bony, but it had filled their bellies. Jack looked across the apple boxes that served as a table. "Did you hear that noise Joe?" The lad looking up, held his breath, Joe shook his head, and said "No I can't hear anything." No sooner had the words left Joe's mouth when there was a loud shout. "Joe! Are you there Lad? Joe!"

Joe , shocked at hearing his Granddads voice, yelled, "Oh Jack! That's me Granddad, I know it is!" He was about to open his mouth to answer, when a fearful Jack shook his head. "Don't call back Joe, not yet, they can't find me, I've got nobody, they'll take me back to Grimthorpe and I'm not going! You go outside, and I'll get down into the cellar. Tell the bobby that I ran off on me own the first day."

Joe was feeling fearful for his pal. "You can come home to Magpies Roost with me Jack. I told you it would be o k. I'm not going without you!" There was a noise outside, and quick as a flash Jack opened the trap door and with a last plea to Joe to keep quiet, he disappeared into the dank cellar.

The search party of three men burst into the cottage. Joe was looking into the face of his Granddad. The boy stood in disbelief for a split second then "Granddad! It's my Granddad, why didn't you come for me? I wanted you, I kept calling you, but you didn't come." Joe cried. Eli and took the lad in his arms, "It's alright now boy don't cry, I'm taking you home."

But Joe couldn't stop the tears. As he left the cottage that had been home for a few days, he feared for his friend. What would happen to Jack? He couldn't leave him to fend for himself, he just couldn't. Joe turned to his Granddad, but the words wouldn't come. He had promised to keep quiet about the cellar, and he must keep his secret, for Jack's sake.

CHAPTER 7

ST CUTHBERT'S HOSPITAL

On the very day that Joe was found there was confusion at the hospital. Mrs Ruth Ford was almost well enough to be discharged. She still had a way to go, but, it had been decided that the woman would fair better in her own surroundings. The mental breakdown was behind her now, she had responded well to the medication, and if only she could have good news of her son, then all would be well. Her specialist along with most other people who knew the story, ruled out any positive conclusion about the woman's husband, and it seemed to everyone involved with her, that she had accepted the inevitable that Reuben Ford was dead. But a blunder was about to take place at St Cuthbert's Hospital, a mishap so unheard of, it would shake the very foundation of that particular theory.

Private 23797 Reuben Ford had been a patient at the convalescent hospital for about five days. In that time, because of the heavy workload, new intakes arriving all the time, the papers relating to each soldier was piling up. In the mayhem that was war, normal practice of knowing the individual history of every patient, was sidelined in order to tend to the needs of the person, Be it soldier, seaman, or airman.

Now, although the convalescent hospital was a separate entity to St Cuthbert's, they did on occasion, share the same specialist. But it was not usual for two patients to share the exact same initials. Mr Patrick Ledbetter, Specialist Neurologist, was attending Mrs Ruth Ford, he hoped for the last time, as the woman was well and truly on the mend. "Well my dear," he said, "and how are we today?" Ruth, sitting out of bed in a chair by the window, gave the doctor a wan smile. "I'm feeling much better thank you Sir." The specialist scanned the papers the nurse had just given him. "What's this nurse?" He flicked the pages. "These notes don't relate to the patient at all. Take them away, and bring the correct papers at once. These belong to the Military kindly send them to the convalescent hospital. By the looks of them, they belong to a soldier, recently arrived. How the hell did these papers get mixed up?"

Ruth noted Mr Ledbetter's annoyance, but she had heard his caustic remarks to the nurses on many occasions. "How, is the soldier in question supposed to be treated when his damn notes are over here?" he continued to rage. Quite frankly, Ruth thought him a pompous know all, but all the same, had to admit he was an excellent doctor.

Had Ruth been aware that the papers in question were the notes relating to her husband's injuries and that Reuben had survived his wounds, and was very much alive, and only a stones throw away. She would not have believed it.

The doctor turned his attention back to his patient. "Well my dear, I think its time you had a little fresh air, how about a few turns around the garden? We must prepare you for your return home." Mr Patrick Ledbetter had a great deal of respect for Mrs Ruth Ford, for against all odds, the woman had fought her way back from near madness. He had seen many go to the wall in similar circumstances, but her drive to regain her health, in order to see her son once more, was to him admirable, and he took his hat off to the woman. It was a great pity her husband had lost his life on the battlefields of France. How he hated this bloody war.

Meanwhile Reuben, unaware of the situation that was about to unfold, was being examined by his doctor. After prodding here, pulling there, Dr Granger seemed satisfied that his patient was on the road to recovery. The doctor looked at medical notes supposedly belonging to the soldier. "Now here's a funny thing Ford, same name, wrong papers, these belong to someone in the main hospital. Somebody with the same initials;." Doctor Granger,hailed a nurse. "See that these notes are delivered to Dr Ledbetter at once."

He then returned his attention to Reuben. "I see no reason why you can't go out into the grounds; a little fresh air will do you a power of good." Reuben smiled his thanks. He was going to be allowed into the grounds along with his pal Alex Weller, who had been bragging about his rides around the grounds with the delectable nurses for some time. He'd made a point that the nurses vied to sit in his knee! Alex Weller was a card, making a joke of the fact that he didn't have a knee to sit on, as both his legs had been blown off just below his bottom. Alex Weller was a man to be admired.

The two soldiers had become firm friends over the past months, giving encouragement to each other when the screaming pain had been unbearable, and the tears of frustration had fallen soft, from eyes that had witnessed horrors unthinkable. Both men glad, one for the other, that they shared something pretty unique. They had both looked death in the face, and beaten it. At the moment, they were enjoying each other's company, taking a turn around the hospital garden, assisted by two nurses, who didn't mind in the slightest. They were very well aware, just what these brave lads had been through, besides, they quite enjoyed the flirting!

As Reuben and Alex trundled along, in the not too comfortable invalid chairs, He was telling his pal about the mix up with the medical papers. "Apparently I got some woman's notes by mistake, a lady in the main hospital, same initials as mine. Funny thing that." Alex, feeling pensive asked, "Aren't they all mentally ill in that place?" Reuben who had tried to make light of the error, felt suddenly strange. "I don't know Alex, and I'd rather not think about that, I was

close to madness myself and I wouldn't wish it on anyone."
And to himself he thought, especially someone with my
initials. But all the same, something niggled in the back of
his mind. Reuben didn't know what, but something was
bugging him. He would ask one of his nurses if she could find
out who the person was. He didn't quite know why he had to
find out, but he needed to know.

It was late summer 1916. As the war raged on, in all its
bloody madness, these two knew that at least, they would no
longer be part of the hell and the killing. For here in this
situation of peace and caring, it was hard to imagine that out
there, young men were dying horribly as war continued to
take its toll. Both men would carry the scars of war forever,
for when the physical trauma had healed, they would be
tormented with images of wanton destruction, and death at its
most horrid. They would eventually find a pocket in their
minds, where they could tuck the hurt away. But now and
again the wounds would need salve, as painful, bitter
memories burned once more.

Reuben and Alex decided to take a turn around the garden, the
wheelchairs where cumbersome, but with a bit of
manoeuvring, and sweet talking the nurses into giving them a
push, they managed to explore the grounds, each time, talking
the nurses into taking a different route.

They had just passed the front of St Cuthbert's, and
disappeared around the side of the building, making their way
back to the 'Wooden Hospital', Reuben's name for the
scattering of huts, as Mrs Ruth Ford was being pushed in a
wheelchair through the main doorway, by a rather large nurse.
"Would you like to sit in the sun dear or do you prefer the
shade?" Ruth, feeling glad to be outside anyway, smiled up at
the nurse, "Oh the sun please, the late afternoon is a lovely
time of day, not too hot., and with smile Ruth thanked the
nurse. Her wheelchair was pushed onto the grass that

surrounded the hospital and just to the west side of the building, in order that the patient could enjoy the last rays of the evening sun.

Ruth settled down by the side of a large weeping willow. This was lovely Ruth took a deep breath of fresh air, and looked around her. She could see part of what she presumed to be the convalescent huts. She could just make out people walking on the lawn. Also there were various people who, like herself, were in wheelchairs. She watched as two patients were being wheeled on to the lawn of the convalescent hospital. They must have been out for a ride. Ruth wondered idly what injuries they would have suffered, and whether they had been wounded in France. Perhaps one of them may even have known Reuben? Little did the lady know that one of patients was her Reuben!

Ruth sighed deeply, she mustn't let herself go down that particular path it was too hard. If she could manage to fill her thoughts with happier things, concentrate on now, and her Dad getting Joe out of that terrible home, instead of wishing for things that weren't going to happen. Then she would be more prepared for going home and building a life, for herself and the Lad. That was how it must be. Her Dad would see that Joe came home. She must believe that.

Her constant prayer, ever since she had known that Joe was living at Grimthorpe Hall had been that her boy would go home to Magpies Roost, where she would eventually join him. Her arms ached to hold her boy. Dear God above, how much longer? She stayed, enjoying the fresh air and late sun, until the nurse came to take her back to Ward 7.

Meanwhile, back at the thatched cottage, the policeman in the search party, who found Joe, fired his gun into the air as a signal to the other searchers that they had been successful. But when Joe told the policeman, and his Granddad, that Jack had in fact run off fearing he would be taken back to Grimthorpe. The mood once again turned sombre. Eli, taking his Grandson gently by the shoulders, asked. "Which way did he go lad?" Joe not wanting to tell a lie, but frightened for his friend, shook his head. "I don't know Granddad." "When did he leave boy? Eli pressed the question. Today, yesterday?" Joe, trembling, tears in his eyes, "I don't know Granddad. I just want to go home." Eli, sensing that the lad wasn't telling the truth and was in fact hiding something, put a comforting arm around Joe. The boy had had enough. Eli turned to the policeman.

"Why don't you leave it with me? The boy's exhausted. Let me talk to him." The Police Constable, noting that Eli Jennings was probably right, nodded his approval. "Alright Eli, get the Lad off home, we'll carry on the search for the other boy in the morning. See what you can get out of the Lad." Eli nodded his thanks to the policeman and the party left the cottage.

When the coast was clear, Jack Simms crawled out of the cellar. He was scared and he didn't fancy being on his own, but Joe had kept his word, he hadn't told on him. Jack was determined that he wasn't going back to Grimthorpe Hall, he'd rather die first! This place was alright, he could make it a home. He could catch fish, there was plenty of fruit and veg and he knew how to cook a stew! Anything was better than Grimthorpe, Mr Sourby and Horrible Horace. No, he was never going back there, ever.

By the time Eli and Joe arrived at Magpies Roost, it was dusk. The day that had been full of mixed emotions had left Joe drained. The lad was trying to deal with so many conflicting feelings. It was lovely to be home, the cottage was as it always had been but it didn't seem real. Even with the familiar smell of stew his Granddad had got going on the stove, didn't tempt him as it once did. So much had happened over these last months, he didn't feel like he used to, there was a sadness he couldn't make better, he missed his Father, and his Mam, and now Jack. What would happen to Jack? Joe could feel the hot tears on his face. Eli, being aware of the anguish in Joe, put a comforting arm around the boy, "Come on Lad, don't take on so, everything will be alright, you'll see." Just then, there was a familiar tap-tap on the kitchen window. Joe held his breath, could it possibly be?

"Kitchener!" Joe cried, "Granddad! It's Kitchener!" Eli nodded, "Yes Lad, he's been here waiting, just like me." Joe rushed outside. The pigeon, recognising Joe at once, cooed and came close. The boy reached out and gently lifted his pal into his arms. The tears that fell on the bird were tears of relief and love. Eli feeling a lump in his throat looked on and sent up a prayer of thanks.

Trouble was, although Joe was home, Eli knew the boy wasn't happy. He'd heard the Lad crying in his bed last night. It was his pal. Joe was worried for his friend, and truth to tell, Eli was concerned for young Jack Simms himself. Joe had talked about his pal and the life he'd had whilst living at Grimthorpe. Apparently he'd been there since the age of three. It seemed that Jack Simms had suffered many a good hiding at the hands of Sourby. Eli shook his head in disgust. Thoughts of what probably happened to the lad disturbed his mind, the poor little blighter, how had he coped? He'd had no one to speak up for him, no mother to love him, not since he was a wee baby. It was heartbreaking.

Eli was reminded of the contretemps he'd had with that swine Sourby, and right now, he felt that given the chance, he would punch the rotten beggar in his fat guts!
Eli was to learn later that Sourby had got the sack from his job and was under investigation for mistreatment of the boys in his care. Talk was that a prison sentence was on the cards.

Mr Andrew Gordon had been given the post of Headmaster of a much-improved Grimthorpe Hall.

Two days after Joe was found, some disturbing news came to Eli's ears. It seemed that the old thatched cottage had gone up in smoke. Jack Simms trying to light a fire, to cook the rabbit he'd snared, set the thatch ablaze. The trouble being there hadn't been any rain for weeks and everything was tinder dry. It was reckoned by the people who had rescued Jack,that a spark from the fire, probably whilst he was cooking some food, had got into the thatch. And that was the end of the old cottage.

Jack was taken to hospital suffering from burns to his hands and face, and smoke inhalation. This being the hardest to treat, causing the boy respiratory problems for quite some time. He was eventually sent back to Grimthorpe Hall. This on the surface wasn't so bad. The Horrible Sourby's had gone, and nice Mr Andrew Gordon was now Headmaster. Conditions were a hundred times better. The boys were well fed and Matron Daphne Crabtree, was given free reign to care for the inmates. It would take time to get rid of all the bad smells that Sourby left behind, but the future, for Grimthorpe Hall, was looking brighter now.

Jack Simms was welcomed back to Grimthorpe Hall by the new Headmaster, and almost at once, the Lad noticed the difference. There was a happier feel to everything, boys, who had known regular beatings, and intense hunger, were actually smiling. Jack thought it was much better now, but he missed Joe. Would he ever see his pal again or, would he have to get used to being without him? Jack thought wistfully of the time he and Joe were the run. It had been exciting. But Joe Ford had gone home to his Magpies Roost, happy to be back with Kitchener, and in his own surroundings. So he must knuckle down and make the best of the new Grimthorpe Hall.

Jack did just that, throwing himself into the new regime now in place at Grimthorpe Hall. Conditions were much better,beating were a thing of the past, food was still tight and plain owing to the war. But the atmosphere in Grimthorpe was homely, just as it should be. But all the same, Jack Simms, hankered after his friend, it wasn't the same without him. They had gone through so much together. Why was life so hard? Would he ever be really happy again?

Joe on the other hand couldn't knuckle down,he was so concerned for his pal. His Granddad had explained about the fire, and Jack being burned and living back at Grimthorpe Hall.
But Joe knew his friend wouldn't like living there again. "Can we go and see Jack Granddad? He won't like it on his own, without me. He said he wouldn't go back there, and they made him, please can we go and get him?" Joe begged his Granddad.

Eli was, by now, very worried about Joe's concern for his friend, he had spoken to Bill Jobson, about the subject. "Thing is Bill, I just don't know what to do. Day and night, the Lad won't give it a rest, wants me to take Jack Simms in. But how can I? Ruth in that place and Reuben God knows where. Dead I shouldn't wonder, has to be, after all these months. No word, no nothing. I tell you Bill, the lad will have me in me grave with all his pining and worrying. He told me yesterday that when his Dad comes home from the war, he will go and fetch the Lad out of Grimthorpe Hall and tell me off for not bringing him home earlier."

The blacksmith had listened with a sympathetic ear. He knew full well how much Eli had struggled to keep the home together. To his mind the old boy had done wonders, considering what he had had to put up with, first loosing Kate to a heart attack, then Reuben, missing 'presumed dead, young Joe, in Grimthorpe Hall, and Ruth, in that God forsaken loony bin, and then there had been Eli's own problems. How much bad luck could one family cope with? Life was unfair and that was a fact. If he tried to make sense of it, he couldn't, there was no rhyme or reason in it.

Bill Jobson loved God. He trusted and feared the Lord, but he couldn't understand him. How could the all seeing, all knowing God, let such things happen to good people? Why was it that the wicked seemed to prosper, while good souls suffered? If there was a message in the suffering, then the blacksmith didn't understand what it was, or why it should be that way. But what he did think was that Eli Jennings had enough on his plate without being bothered with the lad at Grimthorpe Hall.

So Bill listened while Eli opened his heart. "What about taking the boy to see his mother?" He asked, "You know Ruth is improving. It would do her a power of good to see the Lad. Just ask at the hospital, I'm sure it would be alright." Eli was quiet. "I don't know Bill. What about all those mental people and the noises? It's a scary place for a young un?" The blacksmith pondered for a moment. "Well, I think what Joe has gone through lately will have toughened him up and you never know, it may swing things in the right direction. You know as well as I do that this family has had more than their fair share of heartache. The tide has got to turn sometime, come on Eli let's give fate a helping hand, the boy's stronger than you think."

Eli decided that Bill was right. He would grasp the nettle and write a letter to the doctor who was taking care of Ruth, asking if he could take Joe to visit his mother. It was an anxious wait, but when a few days later, a letter arrived back giving permission for Joe to visit. Eli received it with mixed feelings. The letter had stated quite categorically, that the meeting between mother and son would be traumatic, and would need to be treated with kid gloves. After all, they hadn't seen each other for almost eight months, and lots had changed during that time. They had both changed.

When Eli broached the subject to Joe, regarding visiting the hospital to see his Mam, the boy fell silent. Eli, rather perturbed, asked what the matter was. Joe, head bent and shuffling his feet, "I won't know what to say. She'll look different." Eli, worn out with trying to bring up the Lad, and cope with life as it was at the moment. "Don't be silly Boy! She's your mam! We'll go and see her then you'll feel different." Joe, determined to be awkward, "People say that me Mam is in the nut house Granddad! They say she's gone silly." Eli, feeling angry, took hold of the boy's arm. "Now you listen to me my Lad, any more talk like that and I'll tan your arse!" Eli knew exactly what was ailing his Grandson, it was all to do with the fact that Jack Simms had gone back to Grimthorpe Hall, and he was unable to fetch him out, so Granddad was the baddy. The trouble was, as Eli saw it, Joe had lost too much and he was dealing with the anger the only way he knew how. Eli, through gritted teeth," cursed this bloody filthy war."

Eli didn't blame the Lad. Joe was a victim of these terrible times, and all that it implied.
Loss, hardship, anger, children had just as much right to be angry as anyone! They too were suffering in many ways, admitted they didn't know all the horrible details, but nevertheless, war in all its lunacy, touched everybody one way or another.

Bill Jobson suggested Sunday would be a good day to visit St Cuthbert's, he could give the service a miss for once, after all, it would be a Christian act he was doing, almost like that of the Good Samaritan in the Bible. He felt sure he needn't feel guilty for missing church on this occasion.

So on the last Sunday in October, the sun warm enough to be pleasant, the trio set off for the hospital. The journey would take over an hour, but if the weather was fine, then the trip could be quite interesting. The countryside they would be travelling through was breathtaking at this time of year. The kaleidoscope of colour from the trees as they passed by was wonderful, vibrant red and gold turning to purple and silver, defying you to think of war and all its horror.

The beauty of autumn in all its glory allowed you to believe, that yes, God was there.

Everything would be alright one day, and that despite the mayhem, God was still in charge. The horse and trap pulled up out side the main door of the hospital. The journey had taken a little longer, for on the way Joe had wanted to stop off every time they passed a patch of wild flowers. The lad was overloaded with yellow Ragwort, Buttercup and a variety of wild flowers, most now the worst for ware, drooping for the want of water. But Joe clung diligently to his offering.

The horse and trap pulled up outside the main entrance of St Cuthbert's Hospital mid afternoon. Eli, stepped down from the cart, and rubbed his bottom, that was quite a journey and his hip was rather sore. Joe remained seated, gripping the now almost dead flowers. Eli, noting the hesitation in his Grandson, held out his hand. "Come on Lad, we're here now, lets go and find your Mam, she knows your coming."

While Bill tethered the horse to the railing provided, Eli opened the door and stepped inside. On enquiring about Ruth, a care worn looking nurse, in all her uniformed finery, explained that they would find Mrs Ford sitting in the garden under the weeping willow tree. Eli thanked the woman and the three set off to find Ruth.

CHAPTER 8

MEETINGS

Eli could just see the corner of his daughter's wheelchair, almost hidden by the willow tree. As they came closer, Ruth, who had been reading a book' looked up. Eli watched the colour drain from her face. At the same time Joe stepped forward. "Mam, I've brought you these." He handed the wilted bunch of flowers to Ruth, who stared at the boy for a split second, "Joe? My boy, is that really you?" She whispered. The Lad crumpled onto his knees.

"Mam, Oh ,Mam I've missed you so!" Joe begun to cry, and tears that had for so long been heartrendingly sad, flowed with relief. Ruth, overcome, leaned towards her son, "Come here love." Joe, still on his knees, put his head on his Mam's lap and they sobbed together. Ruth caressed her son. To feel him, to touch him was nothing short of a miracle. As she held her boy in her arms, she thanked God for answering a prayer, even when she had been too ill to utter the words.

Eli and Bill, overcome with emotion, wiped away a tear and blew their noses. It wasn't fitting for grown men to cry, but they both cried. Eli suggested that they both take a turn around the grounds whilst Ruth and Joe caught up with everything that had happened to them, over the past horrible months. Joe was to tell his Mam all that had occurred in his life. Ruth would tell very little of what had happened in her own. Joe had suffered too much in his life, without her compounding the situation further, by adding to it.

Ruth listened while Joe told her all about Grimthorpe Hall. The boy endeavoured to leave out the beatings and the cruelty. He had no wish to upset his Mam. Joe Ford had grown up fast over the past months. Ruth was intrigued to hear all about Kitchener, and the part the bird had played in all this, and the tale about Jack Simms was very upsetting, poor little beggar. It was sad that the Lad didn't have anyone at all. Life could be cruel, and that was a fact.

God had seen it in his wisdom to reunite her with Joe, but Reuben was dead, he must be? It seemed to Ruth, that when something good happened, something bad has to happen to balance the books. It was greedy to expect too many nice things at once. But at least now the boy was back with her Dad at Magpies Roost, events would be happier for all concerned.

Ruth hoped that she would soon be going home. She felt sure that the three of them could make a home together, sort of start again from scratch. As far as she was concerned, the thought of her Dad living at Magpies Roost gave her a warm feeling. There was no reason for him to go back to the old home after all it wasn't the same since her mother had died, too many sad memories. Better that her Dad made a home with her and Joe at Magpies Roost. for of course she had no idea that her dad was already there.

The visitors stayed for a good hour, reminiscing and enjoying each other's company. But it was time to make tracks. Joe, who had hardly left his mother's side, seemingly soaking up all the cuddles he had been missing, was loath to leave. Ruth looking and feeling years younger, since holding her son once more smiled at her boy. "It's alright love. You go home, come and see me next week." Then turning to her Dad she said "The specialist dealing with my case, mentioned two weeks, he reckons I will be fit to leave St Cuthbert's by then, barring any mishaps." Eli smiled at his daughter it would be nice to have her home.

Eli looked towards Bill, and with a twinkle in his eye. "I'd better watch out then Bill, tell the young lady who's been keeping me bed warm at night to clear off!" The blacksmith noting a touch of the old Eli shook his head, in mock disgust. It was nice to hear some of the old chap's cheeky banter making a welcome return.

Of course he wouldn't be telling anyone of his delight that Mrs Ruth Ford coming home. He was happy to carry a torch quietly, hide his light under a bushel. He had always been fond of the lass, but he knew she wasn't for him. Ruth had never so much as looked his way. She wasn't aware of his feelings towards her, why should she be? Rueben Ford had married her, and it was obvious to anyone, that she still belonged to Ford, even if he was dead.

Bill Jobson said goodbye to Ruth, promising to bring Joe and her Dad back next week. He walked to where the horse was tethered, untied the reigns and waited until the Lad and Eli had said their farewells. He thought how happy Ruth looked. Well, radiant in fact, it had done the Lass a power of good to see her boy again. The three climbed aboard the trap and set off for home. They reached the corner of the building, and as Joe turned to wave goodbye he heard the sound of a Magpie's chittering call.

"Listen Granddad can you hear the Magpies?" Eli replied. "Yes lad, I can what a racket!" "What do you think is wrong with them Granddad?" Joe asked. Eli smiled, "There's nothing wrong with um lad. Sounds like a feeding frenzy to me. Like as not one of the blighters has caught a young bird, and they all want a bite" Eli smiled at the Lad, how different was his demeanour now, since seeing his mam again. The old man took a deep breath, things would be better from now on. .He could feel it in his bones.

"Come on then, by the time we get home, it'll be time to come back." Eli joked. Joe looked fondly at his Granddad. He was so funny, sometimes he was cross, but Joe didn't mind, being as half the time it was his fault anyway, the other half Granddad said was because of his own old age aches and pains. Oh, and a blasted bunion on his foot! Granddad suffered a lot with his feet.

The horse and trap wended its way along country roads, past a couple of villages and the tiny Hamlet of Thorp End. This consisted of a scattering of dwellings, a small church and a lovely wooded area, a positive haven for a variety of birds. As the horse and trap entered the lower part of the wood, a familiar sound of bird song filled the sweet honeysuckle air. And below the sweetness of song came the chittering call of the magpie. Joe was once again reminded of his father. That familiar feeling of overpowering sadness engulfed him once more. He had seen his Mam, and that was special, she would be coming home to Magpies Roost very soon. But all the time, whatever he was doing, Joe was thinking about his Father. There was an ache deep inside his chest that wouldn't go away.

The party made their way back to Applebee. It was almost dusk when they arrived back at the cottage. Joe hardly gave the horse time to stop, before he was jumping down from the trap, and running to the pigeon loft to make sure his precious Kitchener was alright. He'd had quite a day one way and another, and Joe wanted to talk to his pal about today's events. It had been wonderful to be with his Mam again, Joe thought she looked thinner, and a little older. He loved her. She must come home very soon. He could hardly wait until next week when they would visit St Cuthbert's again.

Meanwhile, Ruth had been making tentative enquiries about Jack Simms. It seemed Joe had been correct about the Lad not having any living relatives and from the way Joe had spoken about the boy the pair had become good pals. She quite understood the sentiment when he had mentioned missing his friend. Something would have to be done about this.

The following week seemed to all concerned, much longer than usual. Ruth could hardly wait to tell Joe and her Father that she would be going home in a few days. Also, further to her enquiries regarding a certain young man, she would be able to give her boy some exciting news

The horse and trap pulled up outside the main entrance. Joe spotted his Mother almost at once, he waved and ran to her, "Hello Mam, how are you today?" Joe could see how she was but it was the right thing to say. Ruth was holding some papers in her hand. Eli who seemed to know what was going on, "You've done it then Lass?" Ruth nodded. "Yes Dad, I've done it!" Joe noting the smile, asked, "What have you done Mam?" Ruth looking happier than anyone had seen her for a long time, "Just you wait and see love, wait and see."

Something was going to happen, Joe could feel it, and there was an expectancy in the air. What was it? His Granddad knew, Mr Jobson knew, why wouldn't they tell him? Just then there was a familiar noise, a loud noise, Joe looked past his Granddad. "It's coming from over there Granddad! I'm going to see." With that, quick as a flash, Joe was running. Eli, feeling his hackles rising, "Come back you young bugger! You can't go over there, it's the military hospital!" Joe, oblivious to his Granddad's call carried on running towards the chittering din. When he was within about 200 yards of the noise, Joe came to a hesitant stop. He could see a group of about four Magpies', high up in the big tree, they were a little quieter now.

But Joe wasn't looking at the birds now! There was something else that had taken his attention. The lawns to the hut hospital, were vast, he could see men in dressing gowns, either sitting in wheelchairs, or reclining on beds. There were nurses either talking to the men, or giving them assistance. But Joe was being drawn towards the tree where the Magpies were perched. He could see two men in wheelchairs sitting under the Magpie tree. Why was his heart beating so fast? He didn't know what, but Joe was experiencing something very odd. He was holding his breath, but he was still breathing in and out. In the background he could hear his Granddad shouting after him, but he was unable to turn round. As he came closer to the two men under the tree, the one with his back to Joe was whispering, "One for sorrow Joe, one for sorrow," and gazing up into the dense branches of the old beech tree.

Joe realised now, why he felt so odd! A miracle was taking place right before his eyes! He couldn't believe it and he stood motionless. With tears choking in his throat, Joe Ford uttered, "Two for joy Father, two for joy." Quick as a flash Reuben turned around. Just for a split second he was struck dumb, Alex Weller seeing the ashen face of his pal, shouted, "In the name of Almighty God, what the hell's wrong with you? Reciting that bloody poem, over and over? I told you it's a bad look verse and no good would come of it."

Reuben, thinking he'd gone mad, shouted back. "Can't you see my boy? He can't be here but he is. For pities sake, help me man!" Reuben let out a piercing scream. "I've gone bloody mad!" Reuben sent up yet another prayer, "God in Heaven, help me!"

Joe in floods of tears now, "Father, it is me, don't cry; please don't cry. Why are you here Father? How did you get to this hospital? Why didn't anyone tell us?" Just then as if that wasn't enough emotion, Eli and Bill came on the scene. The old man, out of puff now from over exerting himself, looked at his Grandson. "What the hell are you playing at Lad? Have you lost your mind? You and your blasted Magpies will be the death of me, and talking to a couple of strangers to boot, you want your arse tanning!" Joe overcome now with emotion shouted out loudly.

"Look Granddad; .It's me Father he's come back! I told you he would!" Joe, snot nosed, tears in his eyes fell against Reuben. The soldier overcome with the realisation that his Son was actually here, took the boy into his arms. "Oh Lad, I've missed you, and you're Mam. Where is your Mam? And what are you doing here anyway?"

Eli was really miffed now, "What the bloody hell is going on here? Who the blazes are you? How do you know Joe?" The soldier then turned his head towards the man whose voice he had recognised. "It's me Eli! Reuben!" Eli scrutinised the soldiers face. "Well, I'll be damned! Good God in Heaven man! How long have you been in this place? Why weren't we told?" Then it hit him! What would he say to Ruth? Come to that, how was he going to tell his son-in-law, that Ruth was within a stones throw of where he was sitting? The old man shook his head in disbelief. This can't be happening! It just can't. Well he needn't have worried, as to how husband and wife would take the strange news.

Joe, sitting up, wiped his nose with his jacket sleeve, "Mam's here as well, Father she's been here for ages. She's with the loony people, but she's not mad."
Eli, doing his best to silence the Lad said "That's enough Joe." But it was too late.
Reuben looked towards his father-in-law, "What's the boy on about Eli? Am I going mad or what? Is Ruth here? For pities sake, tell me!" While Eli tried to explain all that had happened since Reuben had been away at war, Bill hurried back to St Cuthbert's. He would have to tell Ruth something, as to why he was taking her to the convalescent unit, but in Gods name what?

Bill Jobson found Ruth in quite a state. "Where did Joe get to?" Was the first thing she asked The Blacksmith did no more than go to the back of the wheelchair, with the words, "You've got to come with me." He started to push the carriage. Ruth wondered what on earth was going on gripped frantically to the sides of the chair. "What's wrong Mr Jobson? What's happened?" As Bill trundled the wheelchair across the grass, he warned, "You'll see in a minute. Just prepare yourself for a shock."

As they came within sight of the small crowd under the tree, Ruth, recognising her son, called to him. Joe ran towards her almost screaming.

"Its Father! He's here! Look Mam, its Father, he's come home!" The man in question was gaunt, the hair that had almost a year ago been thick and dark brown in colour, was now lifeless and greying, and his lovely eyes, were no longer full of caring, instead they held a look of deep sadness and loss, the twinkle that had once made her toes curl, had disappeared. It was Reuben, but he was a mere whisper of the man, she remembered.

Husband and wife stared at each other. Neither of them could believe what they were experiencing. It couldn't be real. How could this be? It must be a trick, a cruel hoax? Ruth, feeling the blood in her veins running cold, heard her voice speaking, "Is it really you Reuben?" But in her mind she was unable to grasp the truth of what she was seeing.

"Ruth Lass, come here. 'Course it's me." Ruth shook her head, and asked, "Why didn't the army write to me? I waited and waited. I thought you were dead Reuben, dead!" Joe piped up, "I knew you weren't dead, Father, I just knew." Ruth, who could no longer keep the tears from falling, crumpled where she sat. "I can't take this in I just don't believe it's real." Joe rushed to his Mam. "It is real Mam, honest it is. Dad's come home. I told you he would."

It was hard to put into words just how each member of the family was feeling at this very unusual meeting. You may say this sort of thing only occurs in a book, but it did take place.

After all, miracles do happen and they happened for this family. They were going to continue for a little longer. Mr and Mrs Ford were released from hospital within a few days of each other.

CHAPTER 9

COMING HOME

Eli stayed home whilst Joe and Bill travelled the six miles to collect Ruth from St Cuthbert's and bring her back to Magpies Roost. The old man lit the fire. The warmth and the smell of a good rabbit stew would welcome his girl home. Summer days that had been blisteringly hot were beginning to draw in. It was late October 1916. It had been a terrible year. War still raged on the Western Front, and it seemed to some that the mayhem would last forever. Lives had been ruined and people broken, some may never recover from the horror they had endured whilst either fighting the enemy on the battlefield? Or living the nightmare at home? It was debatable who suffered the most.

Ruth Ford, being driven to distraction over the 'Missing, Presumed Dead' telegram, had almost lost her mind. That was the price she had paid for loving! Reuben paid dearly for the love of his wife, son and country. Young Joe had suffered the torment of Grimthorpe Hall, and Eli, he lost his happiness when Kate died. But he had given so much of himself for the love of his family.

The horse and trap drew up outside Magpie Roost. Joe jumped down. "Come on Mam, we're home!" Ruth sat for a moment, and looked around her. Everything looked the same as she remembered, but it felt peculiar, it was home, and yet it wasn't. The yard hadn't been swept for ages and she could see that the garden was overgrown with weeds and dead flowers. There was a sadness, that's what it was, Magpies Roost looked unhappy.

Eli came to the door, "Hello Lass, your home then? Come on, there's a meal in the oven." She stepped inside to the aroma of rabbit stew. Eli turned to the blacksmith, "You'll stay for a bite, won't you Bill?" The man shook his head, "Can't Eli, I've got a couple of horses want shooing. Thanks anyway. Be seeing you Eli." The old man took a deep breath. He had always been aware of the torch Bill Jobson carried for Ruth, the man hid it well, but Eli had always known. It was time the blacksmith found himself a comely lass to warm his bed. The old man had always thought that Polly Armstrong was as likely a contender as anyone. For it was obvious the girl liked the blacksmith judging by the way the girl fluttered her eyelashes at him, and stuck her bosom out every time she saw him!

Ruth sat down and took a sip from the scalding mug of tea her Dad had just handed her, "Dinner won't be long, sit by the fire and get warm." Eli was happy his Lass had come home. Things would soon be back to normal. It wouldn't be long before Reuben was out of hospital. Eli had decided that as soon as Reuben came back, he would go home to his own cottage. He knew that he would be lonely but it was right that his Lass had her own home back. Besides, truth to tell, he'd missed his cottage more than he thought. He was over the numbing pain of loosing Kate now. Anyway, the family were only two doors away.

Ruth set about putting the cottage to rights. Her Dad had done his best, considering what he had gone through himself. But Magpies Roost had lost its sparkle and when her plans came into being, the cottage must be tiptop. So rugs were taken up, thrown over the washing line and given a good beating. Eli had whitewashed the walls of the cottage. Ruth set about cutting up bits of old clothing into equal sizes to make a tab rug for her and Reuben's bedroom. How would she feel sleeping with Reuben again? It had been a long time since she had experienced intimate love, and she didn't quite know how she felt on the subject.

Days turned into weeks, and Magpies Roost was soon looking clean and bright as a new pin. Ruth felt proud everything was in readiness for the return of her Reuben. He would be coming home in a few days, almost four weeks after Ruth had come home to Magpies Roost. She was relieved that at last Joe would have his Father back. The Lad had done his best not to show how much he missed him. But Ruth had realised some time ago, just what it must have been like for her boy living in that awful situation. .

The thought of Joe being in that place filled her with grief. How had he coped?   He was too young to have had such an awful experience. She blamed her own weaknesses for her boy being in that hellhole. Ruth knew Grimthorpe had a bad reputation. But at the time of Joe being placed there, she had had little or no perception of what was going on around her. Nevertheless, Ruth felt responsible for her son's bad experience, and she was determined to make amends.

Joe was showing a great deal of anxiety. He could hardly wait to have his Father back home. But there was something else bothering the boy. Ruth knew what it was, and she longed to let him into the surprise, but she daren't, not yet. It wouldn't be fair if the plan came to nothing.

He had kept himself occupied, as he scrubbed and cleaned the pigeon loft till it almost shone. Kitchener, who now had a couple of lady friends, courtesy of the blacksmith, was strutting around, like a peacock. Apparently he would soon be a proud father! If, the egg that one of his ladies had laid, managed to hatch.

Eli came into the cottage with a letter in his hand. "It's for you love." He said, as he handed the envelope to his daughter.

Ruth wiped her soapy hands down her pinafore. Her mind was working overtime, which one was it? She was expecting two important letters. Ruth, all fingers and thumbs, struggled to open the stiff envelope. "It's from the hospital Dad, Reuben can come home tomorrow! Would you ask Mr Jobson if he could take us?" Ruth was trembling, here it was, the day she had prayed to God for, and she was scared stiff. What would she talk about? Would he be different? What if she had to undress in front of him? How would he be in bed? Perhaps he didn't love her anymore?

It was decided that Eli would stay at home and prepare a hot meal while Ruth and Joe went with Mr Jobson to bring Reuben home from the hospital.

Well, she needn't have worried. The horse and trap arrived at the hospital, and after being informed by hospital staff the correct procedure as to the man's care, Reuben was allowed to go home. The horse, who seemed to feel the happiness trotted at a steady pace, the occupants doing their best to act natural, were making a poor job of it. Joe was the only one who appeared to be happy. Chatting away, telling his Father about Kitchener and his escapades whilst he was resident at Grimthorpe Hall. Reuben didn't quite know how he felt? He should be deliriously happy, he was going home to Magpies Roost. Joe was sat beside him, beaming from ear to ear. And Ruth, his lovely Ruth, smiling relief and love, shining from her face.

But everything was unreal. He had left behind him a place of safety, a place where he was aloud to scream, and weep, and he had said a sad farewell to Alex Weller, his one true friend who had suffered similarly to himself in this hellish war. The man was all alone. No family to call his own. How would the man cope? Reuben knew he was going to miss the chirpy Yorkshire man. Reuben also carried with him, scars that would take a long time to scab over. Trouble with scabs, there was always the temptation to pick at them, meaning, they took longer to heel. But Reuben knew some wounds would never really get better, picked at or not. They festered in the frequent nightmares, turning him into a sweating, frightened wreck. But they do say that time is the healer. Reuben would wait and see.

The blacksmith pulled his horse to a gentle halt outside the door of Magpies Roost, Joe jumped down from the cart. "Granddad, we're back! Father's home!" Eli came slowly to the door, grubby cloth in hand. Reuben climbed gingerly from the trap.

"Hello Lad, nice to have you back where you belong." Eli took his son-in-laws hand.

"Come on in. I've just taken the rabbit stew from the oven, you look as though you could do with a good meal."

Reuben couldn't eat very much. The stew was nice but he hadn't the stomach for it. Perhaps when he got used to being home he would regain his appetite. Eli certainly hoped so, for he had welcomed a skeleton back to Magpies Roost. Ruth and Reuben treated each other with kid gloves, neither of them knowing quite how they should be with each other. They were polite, one to the other, but nothing seemed to come natural, or spontaneous as it used to. Ruth worried that the change in Reuben would be permanent. Reuben worried that he couldn't be a husband to his wife. Not yet anyway. The horror he'd witnessed in France was still at the back of his eyes, he saw something of the carnage every time he closed them. Thank God Ruth would never have to see what he saw, or witness what he had seen.

Did Joe notice the change in his Father? He must have done. But the Lad was so glad to have him home. If he had thought his Father had changed he hadn't mentioned it. What the Lad had been happy to talk to his Father about though, was Kitchener, and everything that had happened to them both, whilst he'd been at Grimthorpe Hall, the pigeon had done wonders. Reuben was able to detect that, from the things Joe was telling him, it was obvious that Joe loved Kitchener, and strangely, the bird seemed to have real affection for the boy. Stranger things had happened between man and animal. Why shouldn't it? We don't know everything. After all, doesn't it say in the Holy Bible 'and the lion shall lie down with the lamb?' This somehow comforted Reuben.

Joe told his Father about Jack Simms, and the friendship they had shared. Reuben detected sadness in his Lad when talking of his pal, he also realised that he hadn't been the only one to suffer in this hellish war. All had struggled one way and another.

A few days after Reuben's return, a letter arrived from Grimthorpe Hall telling Ruth that her request had been granted. She had kept quiet regarding her plans, in case they didn't come to fruition. She had discussed the idea with Reuben and her Dad, but not Joe. But it was time now to let Joe into the surprise.

"You mean Jack is coming here to live with us? Oh, Mam!" Joe, arms around his Mother, "When is he coming Mam? When?" Ruth tears running down her face, "He'll be here shortly. Mr Jobson and your Granddad have gone to bring the Lad home." Joe, overcome with emotion, kissed his Mother, and held her tight. "Thanks Mam. But how do you know he wants to come and live here?" Ruth explained to Joe her concern for the orphan after listening to her son's story about the boy. "Anyway Joe, its obvious you two got on, and you were missing the boy. So I got in touch with Mr Andrew Gordon, the new Headmaster of Grimthorpe Hall, and he agreed that Jack should come and live with us, as he doesn't have a family of his own. He told me all about your exploits when you were together, and he did say that Jack was fretting ever since you left. And when asked if he would like to come and live here, he said yes, so papers were signed and that was that."

The horse and trap pulled up outside Magpies Roost. Eli and Jack Simms stepped down into the yard. As they did so Joe noticed a flock of four Magpie settle on the tree at the back of the cottage, "Look Father, can you see? Four Magpie."

"One for sorrow, two for joy, three for a girl, four for a boy." Reuben said.
"Its good luck Father, three for a girl and four for a boy. That means Mam and Jack, it must be magic!" Ruth and Reuben looked at each other and smiled. The Magpie rhyme had always been special to Joe and Reuben, Ruth understood in part, what the poem meant to the pair. She had always known of the rhyme, somebody had written it years ago. There were a few variations of the poem. Her mother used to spout the Yorkshire version when Ruth was a girl. The words always amused Kate.

Joe rushed to meet his pal. Jack, looking rather awkward, gave Joe a shy smile. "I didn't know I was coming to live along with thee?" Joe laughing at the broad Yorkshire twang, "Come on Jack, I'll show you our bedroom." Jack carrying all he possessed in a cardboard suitcase, followed his pal into Magpies Roost, and a wonderful new life.

Life at Magpies Roost in the village of Applebee was a mostly a happy place now. Strange how the old rhyme, that had meant so much to Reuben and Joe, had, during these difficult times, been the cement that had held them together. Wonderful things do happen, and they were about to happen once more. Reuben had been in communication with his pal Alex Weller, ever since he had come home. By the tone of his friend's letters, Alex was in a bit of a quandary. The man felt his life was finished, no prospects, no family, and worst of all, no legs! Reuben had discussed his concerns about his friend to Ruth and Eli, and a solution had been found, if Alex agreed. Reuben was awaiting a reply to his letter.

Just before Christmas, 1916, Alex Weller moved in with Eli. It had been decided that as Eli had gone back to his own cottage, when Reuben had returned home, that the solution was clear. Eli had the space, he was able to climb the stairs now to his own bedroom, if he took it steady, leaving the spare bed downstairs for Alex. Besides, he'd met the legless Yorkshire man and he liked him, they would be company for one another.

So while the war, that was causing so much misery to so many, was to rage on for another two years, bringing in its wake more heartache and misery. This little band of troupers would make the best of a bad job. They'd all come through some pretty tough time's one way and another, but they were all alive, and they had each other. War makes men of some and cowards of others. The latter certainly didn't apply here.

Reuben was to find employment with Bill, the blacksmith, Eli and Alex enjoyed an occasional drop of the hard stuff, Joe and Jack got up to plenty of mischief, Kitchener fathered two baby pigeons and was treated like royalty by his loving owner. And Ruth, well, she oversaw everything, threatening to tan the boys' backsides more than once for their misbehaviour, especially when they sang the Yorkshire version of the old rhyme!

One for sorrow
Two for joy
Three for a girl
Four for a boy
Five for silver
Six for gold
Seven for a tale never to be told
Eight you live

Nine you die
Ten you eat a bogey pie!

Lightning Source UK Ltd.
Milton Keynes UK
UKOW03f1813141014

240098UK00001B/65/P